Ghosts of Wyoming

D0974190

Other books by Alyson Hagy

Snow, Ashes
Keeneland
Graveyard of the Atlantic
Hardware River
Madonna on Her Back

GHOSTS
OF WYOMING

Stories

Alyson Hagy

Graywolf Press

Publication of this volume is made possible in part by a grant provided by the Minnesota State Arts Board, through an appropriation by the Minnesota State Legislature; a grant from the Wells Fargo Foundation Minnesota; and a grant from the National Endowment for the Arts, which believes that a great nation deserves great art. Significant support has also been provided by the Bush Foundation; Target; the McKnight Foundation; and other generous contributions from foundations, corporations, and individuals. To these organizations and individuals we offer our heartfelt thanks.

Published by Graywolf Press
250 Third Avenue North, Suite 600
Minneapolis, Minnesota 55401
All rights reserved.

www.graywolfpress.org

Published in the United States of America

ISBN 978-1-55597-548-7

2 4 6 8 9 7 5 3 1
First Graywolf Printing, 2010

Library of Congress Control Number: 2009933819

Cover design: Scott Sorenson

Cover art: Michael Hall, Getty Images

For Connor
Spirits & Stories

Contents

Border

It was not as hard to steal the collie pup as he thought it would be. From early morning when the woman set up and wiped her table with a cloth until the time the silver container of coffee was emptied by those coming to look at the dogs, there had been somebody around the camper and around the crate that held the pups. But lunch hour put the scatter in people. Tacos and fry bread were for sale on the other side of the bleachers—he could smell them. And the heat slowed things down, even for the dogs that panted hard and fast like they knew they were destined for the sheepherding finals.

The high sun was what seemed to drive the woman into the camper. It was nothing more than company, the chance to talk out of the hearing of adults, that got rid of the girl and her sister. They went off with kids they seemed to know from the sheep-raising universe of Colorado. There was discussion of buying Cokes or lemonade. The older girl was the one who'd offered him a pup to hold.

He'd refused, staying polite and not looking too interested. He had a dog at home, he said, one that was good over pheasant and jumping in the water for ducks. A hunting dog from Texas. This was a lie from his mouth, though he'd heard the exact same words said by a long-haul friend of his father's.

Except for the dog stories, he had not liked that friend.

The girl had smooth brown hair held off her neck in braids the way 4-H girls he knew wore their hair, especially the ones who barrel raced on horses. He was a little sorry she would get in trouble because of him. She'd take the blame, no matter what. That was how it worked. But there was a pile of pups in that crate. At four hundred dollars apiece, nobody's feelings or whipped ass was going to hurt for long.

Luck would determine if it was male or female. He wouldn't have time to check. A bitch was easier to train. This, too, came from his father's friend. But there was some number of male dogs in the finals. He'd watched them stalk the skittery bands of sheep in the preliminaries. He knew how capable they were. And he didn't care what it was. The one the girl held away from her chest to show him had looked good enough to him. Everybody knew border collies were smart beyond the ordinary for dogs. You could train them to within an inch of their business, and they would wait outside a building for you with no rope or leash. They would wait for you all day.

He partly zipped his jacket and snapped the snap on its waistband. His Broncos hat was already so low on his head he could barely see. He slipped in and unpinned the crate before he even squatted down. The lucky one was toward the front, round bellied, asleep on its side. He used two hands for support so as not to shock the pup, wanting it to think well of him from the get-go. He lifted it like it was a glass tray. Then he got one hand under its sleepy, dangled haunches and slid it into his jacket. It didn't make a peep, nor did its many sisters and brothers. He closed the crate, put a quick touch on the bill of his Broncos hat to be sure it was set square on his head, and he was gone.

He waited until he was clear of the Meeker Fairgrounds to take off his jacket and turn it inside out so that the brown cloth fabric showed instead of the blue. He also removed his hat and tucked it into his back pocket, though his bare head felt show-offy to him. This was his disguise. He had to set the pup on the ground to make his changes. It was more alert now, and he saw its tongue bend in an arch when it yawned, and he saw its tiny teeth. The teeth were see-through and small like fish teeth. He scooped the pup with his hands and cradled it. It was a female. He could tell that much. He could also tell from the mask of her face that she had the good, preferred markings he'd heard the handlers talk about.

She made a sound in her white-furred throat, and he made a sound back.

He carried her through town inside his brown jacket, cars and trucks passing on both sides of the road. He supported her round belly with his hands, walking as if his hands were only in his jacket pockets and he was only going for a stroll. He used sidewalks when he could. He wished he could stop at the cafe he saw—one with yellow paint around the windows—but he knew he could not, even though he had money, because of the deputies and what had happened with his father. He read the sign for the cafe that hung out over the street, and he liked the sound of the name. Belle's. He could call the pup that, call her Bell after the instrument and after the cafe in the town where he'd gotten her. Border collies always came with short names. It cut down on confusion.

Bell. A good name for a dog that was bound to be sweet but never shy.

He walked until he got to the gas stations. There was one on each side of the road just before the road filled out into a highway. He saw what he hoped to see on a good-weather Sunday, a steady stream of livestock trailers and open-backed trucks, many of them too large and awkward to pull next to the pumps. He'd planned to buy food, but he knew better than to pass on what looked like a rare chance. A red trailer stacked with hay was goosenecked to a diesel pickup with Colorado plates. The driver had left the rig angled near the air hose. He did what he'd done before, apologizing to Bell in a low voice for the delay of their supper. He unlatched the trailer's gate on one side and stepped into the dark crowdedness of the hay. Then he slid Bell loose from under his jacket and set her safe in the trailer's corner. He turned, made a loop of the orange rope that was already tied to the rear of the trailer, caught the latch handle in that loop, snugged the gate closed, and dropped the latch to lock them inside. It would be a hell of a sight easier to travel with hay than with steers or horses. They might not even get caught.

He sat down and drew Bell onto his lap, leaning into the sweet wall of hay. Bell had slept in the nest of his jacket, but she was awake now. Her dazedness was wearing off. He could feel the difference in the set of her legs and the sharp probing of her teeth on the soft parts of his hands. She would miss her brothers and sisters soon. He knew how that would go. Missing a sister— he did not have a brother—was a burn that was slow to cool. What he needed most was for Bell not to bark. Barking would not be good. He tried to keep her busy chewing on the bottoms of his jeans and on his hands, though her sharp fish teeth were already making him sore. He was glad when the driver cranked the rig and they eased onto the highway. The weather was dialed in. There would be no problems with heat or cold. They could find food later. He understood food was something he had learned to do without while Bell had not. But if he was right, the trailer's destination was close—no more than a couple of hours. He pulled his Broncos hat from his pocket and smoothed it down over his hair. He knew how to wait.

When the rig slowed to leave the highway, he took a look and thought the town might be Hayden. The driver pulled into another gas station but didn't cut the engine—it seemed like the driver only needed to take a leak. He bundled up Bell and got out of the trailer while the going was good. The sun was still flat and clear in the sky, but the air was beginning to smell of evening. He walked behind the station and took a leak of his own, then he let Bell walk and sniff some in the gravel. He needed to get one of those whistles, the kind only a dog could hear. For now, he'd count on his voice and the way Bell would learn to listen to it.

"Come on, Bell. Come on, little gal." He knelt on the gravel and called until she came to him. He told her she was pretty smart to make him proud on her first day.

He apologized for what he had to do next. He set her in an empty barrel that was soured from garbage, and he walked fast around the station and went inside and bought a pint of milk and some sticks of peppered jerky and two bottles of the fancy water his father made fun of. He paid for his selections with the bills folded in his front pants pocket. He was tight with worry for Bell. He got back, and he stroked her on top while she drank water from a hamburger container until they both were calm. There was hay mixed in her black fur and a flat mark of grease on her tail. He tried to clean her with his fingers. He had some water, too, while Bell lapped at the milk, then he got after the jerky. Bell didn't care for the jerky. He told himself that next time he would get the kind without pepper.

He had passed through Hayden before, and he liked his chances of finding a ride. He knew people paid no attention to strangers and how they came and went, alone or not alone, in the summer. He only wondered how bold he should be. His question was answered by the arrival of a club cab Ford bearing two cowboys. He was standing near the phone booth when it pulled in.

He watched the driver for a short time. The driver was a rodeo cowboy, for sure. Ironed shirts hung in the window of the Ford, and there was a show hat on the driver's head. The passenger was dressed cowboy, too. He walked up to the driver and asked for a ride.

"It's just me and this little dog," he said.

The driver, who was young and red skinned from the day's sun, looked him over. "Where to?"

"I got cousins on the Front Range, cousins and a aunt," he lied. "Anyplace toward Denver is good. The dog is for them."

"Denver it is," said the driver.

"Tell him he's got to buy beer." This came from the passenger.

"I don't believe he's old enough to buy beer."

"Shit. You know what I mean."

"I got money," he said. And he dug into his pocket with some defiance. He freed up ten dollars, handed it to the young driver.

"Cute dog."

"She is," he said. "Smart, too."

"What if she messes in the truck?" This from the passenger again, in a mood.

"I'll hold her. If she wets, she'll wet on me."

"I got a towel," the driver said. "I don't know what Ray's worried about. A little dog like that can't outmess him nohow."

"Fuck you," said the passenger, making one piece of a smile. "And give over that money. I've got a thirst."

They got going pretty fast, him and Bell squeezed in the back of the cab with some rigging and a bull rider's vest. He held Bell so she could look out the window as they drove, and she seemed to like that. The driver and Ray cracked beers and drank them and didn't talk. They started to talk when they slowed to pass through Steamboat Springs because they wanted to make fun of the town for its traffic lights and tourists. The driver said he didn't know a single good horseman who could still afford to live in Steamboat.

"They got girls, though," said Ray. He was watching out the windows just like Bell.

"Not the kind you like," said the driver.

"What's that mean?"

"It means rich. It means talking and spoiling and taking your time."

"And I can't do that?"

"Besides the fact that you're butt ugly, I've never seen you slow down for nothing, not even a rich girl."

"Fuck you."

"It's true," the driver said, laughing. "We have plowed this field before—"

"I ain't plowed nothing with you. You can't—"

"My point is you could act right with girls, but you don't."

"And who are you? Mister Smooth Shit?"

"I didn't say one way or the other. I didn't say a thing."

Ray looked over his shoulder. "You say you're giving up that dog. I wouldn't give up a good dog or a good gun, neither one. With dogs and guns you know what's next. They stay in bed all damn night whether you want them or not."

"You got to excuse Ray," the driver said, laughing some more. "He just got throwed off the crippledest mare on the Western Slope."

"You didn't do so hot yourself, twig dick."

"I didn't. It's lucky I got a credit card for gas."

They went into their third beers as the truck hauled up Rabbit Ears Pass. He stashed their empties at his feet. Bell whined some at the change in altitude until Ray asked to hold her. He didn't want to give her up, but he knew travel meant all range of favors. So he gave Ray the pup, and she seemed to take to him, working at his skin and his sleeves with her tongue and teeth. Ray gave him a cold beer in return, and he drank it, grateful.

He would guess later that it was the losing Ray couldn't get past because he couldn't find anything else about the situation that might have flipped the switch. Ray hadn't had that much beer, none of them had. It was just that Ray had to make somebody else the loser.

"This is a nice dog," Ray said after Bell curled into his lap for some sleep. "How old?"

"Seven weeks," he said. "She still misses her mama."

"I don't miss mine. How much she cost you?"

He paused, listening for the trap. Older boys and men liked to set traps. "Four hundred," he said.

Ray made a whistle sound behind his lips. It was not the admiring kind. The sound perked Bell up. "How much did those heelers go for in Rifle?" he asked the driver. "I saw Bobby Byrd take one, but I don't recall the price."

The driver turned his head for one second. "I don't remember, had to be a couple hundred. You know, when you wake a pup—"

"Oh, damn. Shit."

"That ain't shit."

"Damn. Make her stop. Come on, dog, stop."

"Naw," the driver said, laughing once again. "Your britches ain't wet with shit."

Ray cussed a long streak, holding Bell in the air like a paper airplane while he tried to work the piss off his legs. The towel, they'd all forgotten that. The driver, still aiming fast into the valley, reached under his seat and found an oil rag, which he tossed at Ray. "Oh," said the driver. "Oh, I got one now. Pissed pants and a crippled mare. I got a story to tell on you now."

"Goddamn dog," Ray said. "Right on my good jeans."

"I'll take her," he said from the backseat. "She didn't mean to hurt nothing."

"The hell she didn't," Ray said. "She's one bad thing after another on a bad day. So are you. Dillon there made you part of my damn bad day."

"Then let us off," he said, his heart bolting the way it did when he was close to trouble. "That's what you can do."

"That's not what I *want* to do," yelled Ray.

"Christ, Ray," said the driver. "It's no more than pup piss. It'll dry."

"It is more. It's what you said."

"Christ, then. I take it back. I didn't mean to get under your saddle."

"Yeah, you did, you son of a bitch. In the money at Gunnison two weeks ago and you ain't let up since. You don't think I'm good enough to haul with your goddamn gear."

"Give the kid his dog."

"No."

"Give it to him."

"I'll give him something else first," Ray said, his hand going after his belt buckle, and that meant two things to him in the backseat—it meant belt whipping or worse—and he'd given up taking the hurt of both, so he reared between the seats and grabbed for little Bell. But Ray was quicker, and mean. Ray kept his hands free, and he got his window down, and he dropped the dog out onto the moving road.

"Christ. Jesus Christ, Ray. You can't do that," yelled the driver. But he had.

The driver, Dillon, hit the brakes, which sent them all flying forward and cut down on the punches and kicks that followed. They threw him out of the truck, too. Ray kept yelling, his face the color of meat, but he heard nothing of it. He ran. He was all running. He saw her by the side of the road, black and white like a shoe tossed into the bristly cheatgrass. He saw her move. Then he was by her and with her, lying on the ground low and flat so she might see his face. Pleading. "Don't be dead, Bell. Please don't be dead."

She staggered to her feet. She shook her head as though her ears itched, then bounded deeper into the bristled grass. She went away from him and away from the road. Scared.

"She rolled. Swear to God she rolled, I saw it in my mirror. She might be all right." It was the driver, Dillon. He had backed his truck up to where they were. Ray wasn't with him. "Young ones like that don't have much bone. She might not've felt it."

He lifted her up, afraid to see blood in her mouth, afraid she'd have eyes like his sister's cats after they had been drop-kicked.

"I'd take you to a vet, but I can't, not with Ray. I'm sorry. The town's right up here. Walden. I'm sorry. Here's money to have her looked at."

There were sounds. The truck disappeared. He made out that the truck stopped for Ray before it started again, and he made out the pale leaf of a twenty-dollar bill on the darkness of the road. He picked up the bill and put it in a separate pocket. Bell's heart was like a hammer against his hands, and his own heart was moving blood so fast it made his stomach sick. He was afraid the live part of Bell would tear through the skin of her chest and leave him behind, but it didn't.

After a minute or two she acted like she wanted to walk. He didn't let her down at first, but then he did. She walked like normal. She sniffed at the oily road. When she saw a grasshopper and tried to stalk it, he knew she was all right. Bent, but not broke. He told her he was glad. That he was proud of how tough she was and how she learned things. What she'd learned was a lesson he hadn't meant to teach her right away even though it was the kind of thing that was bound to come before you were ready for it, the black lesson of fear.

He let her play until his face was dry.

There were lights in some of the Walden houses, and the air was as cool as the river. The streets were quiet. He and Bell weren't likely to catch a ride now. He walked along the main street where the businesses were closed until he saw a pizza place. It was open, and there were kids inside, regular kids, paying $7.95 for the special advertised in the window. He wished he could spend his money that way. Maybe when they got to Denver he would. As a treat for himself even more than Bell.

He walked past the pizza place with Bell snug in his jacket. He turned left, smelling hot bread, then turned left again at the alley. The dumpster was near the kitchen where he could hear people talking and banging things as they worked. After dark, he would check the dumpster. Leftover pizza wasn't bad if you got it out of the box quick.

If a deputy or anybody asked, he was waiting for his father who was fishing. There was a lot of fishing around Walden. He knew that even though he was from across the state line in Wyoming and had only been fishing with his father one time that he remembered.

His mother had never been part of anything.

He started walking again to avoid deputies and the kids moving through the spreading dark on their bikes. This was how he found the funny house. To him it looked no bigger than a garage with windows, and it was painted orange with trim that had some purple parts and some red. It was the kind of place that made people shake their heads. There was a white fence, too, no higher than his knees, and a small sign on the fence written in swirly letters. He put Bell down along the fence while he tried to read the letters. This was when she started to talk.

"Is that you, Donny? Donald Bunch? Is that you raising money for the band?"

The woman was at the purple door of the house. She was holding on to the door frame with both hands.

"No, ma'am. It's not who you think."

"Are you coming in? We're still open."

"I don't know. I just got here. I have my dog."

"You should come in," she said, turning. "I'm not busy. I like dogs."

He got Bell from the ground, and he opened the gate in the

low fence and went in. He wanted to be polite. The woman stopped him at the screen part of her door and said again how much he looked like Donny Bunch or any of the Bunch brothers.

"Do you know him from school? He lives on Spur Ranch. Likes to ask me for money."

"No, ma'am, I don't know him. I'm not from here."

"Just as well," she said. "New faces mean new facts. Come in so I can see you."

He thought then that there was something wrong with her eyes and the way they seemed not to look right at him. He wondered if she was blind or partly blind. He was still wondering when he went into the house that smelled like a flower shop that kept both old flowers and new ones. The front room was crowded at the edges. There were square tables of different heights. There were books and piled magazines.

"Do you have a name?"

"I do. Tyler. Tyler . . . Bell."

"And your dog?"

He realized his mistake. "She don't have her right name yet, I just got her."

"We might have to give her one then. She's very pretty," the woman said, touching Bell between the ears like she knew what she was doing. Like she wasn't all blind. "Will you have something to drink? We're open."

He could tell there was no other person in the house to make up a "we." He wasn't sure what it would cost to drink something. He didn't see any lists. But he would pay if he had to. Ever since smelling that pizza, he'd wanted to spend money.

"I can't stay long," he said. "But a soda is okay if you have some."

"Would tea be all right . . . and water for your friend? I have that. I'm sorry to hear you're in a hurry. You didn't look it."

He started to tell the story about waiting for his father but something made him stop. He said nothing rather than saying a lie. His father hated places like the funny house. He would hate the woman and say terrible, rude things to her. But now . . . now he was a long distance from his father. He had changed how the two of them were. Thinking of that made his hands go thick and hot.

The woman came back with water in a dish for Bell. Her return stirred up the smells again, the papery thin ones he didn't know. Bell was all over the floor of the house, playing, but it seemed to be working out. The woman said tea would be ready soon—he could have any kind he liked—and she apologized for the noise of a radio he'd barely heard.

"It's the war," she said. "Sometimes I can't stop listening to it."

He looked at her and her funny eyes when she said that. There was something in them, or not in them. "Do you have somebody over there," he asked, "in that war?"

"No, Tyler, I don't. My boy fights what he fights down in Pueblo. I don't see him very much. I'm listening because I think if I listen long enough I can learn what a damn thing is about. They've got me fooled on that. I still think there's an answer to my questions. Maybe you'd like to tell me I'm wrong."

"No, ma'am," he said. "I wouldn't do that."

"You're shy," she said. "But I can tell that doesn't keep you from taking care of yourself."

"The pup," he said. "I'm taking care of her."

"Yes. I see that. You're very good with the dog."

Then there was tea—he picked a mint one—and milk to put in it and lemony cookies and peanuts in a clay bowl. He ate more than he should have. He let her see he was hungry, but he planned to pay her so there would not be an obligation. He liked how she did everything calm and slow, though after a while it was hard for him to keep from yawning.

While he drank tea, the woman lit a match and put it to a

straw she took from a bunch of straws. She stuck the straw in the pot of a green plant, and it gave off sweet smoke that he watched curl into the air.

"It's called a joss stick," the woman said, knowing he was watching it.

"Joss. It smells good," he said.

"I had a cat named Joss," she said. "A good cat. I don't suppose the name would do for a dog."

"It might," he said. "I could think about it."

"How old are you?" she asked.

"Fourteen," he said. And that was the truth.

Night darkened the windows of the house until he saw the two of them in the separated panes of glass. She was smaller than he was, and careful moving with a thin cap of white hair, and seeing that made him ashamed that he'd forgotten to remove his Broncos hat. He was double ashamed he hadn't asked for her name. It felt too late to do it now.

He said, "I should take this pup and go on."

"Oh," she said, clearing his plate. "You're ahead of me. You're making a move, and I haven't even asked you to stay."

The air around him closed in with all its smells, then opened again to his hard breathing. He took Bell onto his lap not knowing what to say.

She said, "I appreciate your not fooling with me. You have character. You haven't asked for a thing. But I know you're on your own, I can see that much. It's cold out, or it will be, and you need a place to sleep."

He sat in the chair she'd given to him, thinking. There was a bladed feeling in his stomach. He wanted to dull that blade and keep it sharp all at once. After a long minute he asked if she was a schoolteacher.

"I have been a teacher. I've been a lot of things, some of them good, some just necessary. You don't have to worry, I won't ask you many questions."

"Just a few."

"A few. Yes."

Bell was wiggling to get down. He stood, planning to walk out.

"The dog," the woman said. "She shouldn't be in that cold without a name or a bed. You need to think of her."

He cleaned himself at her sink and put on a sweatshirt she had given him. The shirt was soft and faded. He wondered if it belonged to her son. There was a box for Bell with rags and paper. For him, there were blankets the woman brought from downstairs. It looked like she slept there, in the basement. She said he could sleep on the floor next to Bell.

"It's not like home," she said.

He said, "It's real nice. Thank you."

"I call it home," she said, seeming to chew around the word. "That's my name for what it's made of me."

After the woman left, Bell lay down in her box, and he sat upright and watched her breathe for a long time. He liked how her body was loose. He liked how the day hadn't left any marks on her. He touched her a few times on the head before he lay down to make himself loose. The house was warm, and it felt smaller than ever, like a tight, lidded box. He wondered if his breath, and Bell's, and the sad, stretched breathing of the woman could fill up the box in a single night.

They were at the door before he was awake. There was one at first, a deputy, and then another one. He was confused from sleep and from how quickly the woman walked around him and around Bell like she could see fine in the dark. She didn't say anything. It wasn't even morning. Bell shook herself like dogs do. She started licking at her fur with her tongue while the inside of him took off running at full speed, his heart and his head—flying at full speed. The rest of him stayed put, stiff and silent next to Bell. It was too late.

The woman tried to talk to the deputies through her door, but they came in, two of them dressed in uniforms and thick jackets. He stayed on the floor with his legs held straight under the blankets so they could see he'd quit. When one of them said his real name, he nodded. He knew they'd seen copies of his picture.

"You come along with us," the first deputy said. "We know you got a story. We don't want trouble."

He nodded again. Asked if he could put on his shoes.

"Not until we check," the first one said. "Stand up and let us check."

They stood him up and put on handcuffs and took the money from his pockets and took his hat, and while they touched him in those ways, his mind went to a high, cool place where it could stand hours of dark and hours of light and still hear the occasional hopeful words if they were spoken. He knew how to quit. And he knew how not to quit on everything. The thing he would miss most was Bell. He'd really wanted it to work out with her.

The woman was talking faster than her usual talk. With more letters and sharp notes.

She said, "I didn't ask questions. But I know a thing or two, I figured you out."

He stood there wearing her soft sweatshirt, not able to give it back.

She looked at him with padlocked eyes. "It's the kind of person I am. What I've turned into. I made a clear decision."

He asked, "Will you take care of her?"

"I can't."

"I wish you'd thought of her. She likes it here. I guess I don't think it's right not to think of her, a little dog, when you make a decision. That's how you said it with me. You said I had to consider." He remembered how Ray had thrown Bell out of the truck and how he'd never told the woman about that. Maybe it would have made a difference to her, that story.

She said, "You made your decision when you put your father in a pool of blood up there in Lyman, Wyoming. It might have been right to do that. I don't know. Things get out of order in a family. Living gets us out of order."

He climbed upward to his safe, inside place, hand over hand. The woman went on, and the deputies went on, and they laid out their sentences like smooth, straight roads telling about his sister and who was caring for her and what his chances were. Bell left her box and came to his feet. She scratched at his jeans with her claws until the second deputy picked her up.

He said, "Cute dog."

The woman said, "You let him ride with that dog, Walt Mason. You let him have her in the car for the drive to where you're going. He won't see her again."

He heard what the woman said in his high, quiet ears. She *had* been a schoolteacher, it was all through her voice. He was glad to know that. She had been a teacher in another time and another world that never included him, maybe a world that worked better than his did. She had taught things he hadn't learned. Still, he knew little Bell would be good for the woman, he felt that, everybody in the tiny house had to feel that, and the woman didn't want the dog. He didn't understand. He would never understand, not with any carving of his heart he wouldn't. How could anybody not want the thing that would keep them from being sent backward one last time?

Brief Lives of the Trainmen

The Callboy

He is awake before daylight greases the black pan of the sky. The cook rouses him with the ring of her iron ladle across the brake spring. He hears the cook curse her rheumatic gout, the withholding chickens, the moths that have drowned in her uncovered pots. Her voice is as complaining as a crow's. He worms his feet into the square-toed brogans left behind by the spike setter who caught gold fever from a bullwhacker out of Rapid City. The brogans are too large, but he'll keep them until he can trade for something better. He bundles his spare shirt and stockings with the grain sack that is his bed, then reties the rope that belts his woolen trousers. The rope is a gift from the cook. She used it to lead the pig before she butchered him.

He tucks his belongings under one arm and shimmies open the boxcar door. The morning smells of mule and tar. The surveyors' tents, set like a widow woman's teacups on the flat plain to the south, are barely visible against the chalky soil he can taste when the wind blows his way. The surveyors will snore until their biscuits are baked. They aren't his worry. It's the first shift he's after, the gangers who sleep too late in summer, except for the Chinese. The Chinese aren't his worry either. They take care of themselves.

He jumps to the roadbed in his gentleman's shoes.

When he reaches the first of the boarding cars, he finds Mr. Donahue preparing to piss onto the link and pin. The gang boss has forbidden this practice, which only makes it more pleasurable and frequent. He likes Mr. Donahue, who signed the payroll as Mr. Garrity the month before, and Mr. Haughey the month before that. Mr. Donahue is free with his pennies. "Morning, scalpeen. Are ye seeing the men to their labors?"

He nods. It is the same every morning save Sundays, when Mr. Donahue seldom cracks an eye before noon.

"Good on ye," says Mr. Donahue, unbuttoned, steaming. "I'll utter me first prayers here."

The Hotel-on-Wheels

There are three boarding cars, three tiers of bunks each. The Chinese, who aren't allowed in the cars, make camp nearby, though never among the surveyors. The callboy monkeys his way up the grab bars and swings into the stink of the first car still lugging his belongings, which he hopes to leave under the blanket on Billy Dolph's bunk. Farts, oil of Macassar, whiskey distilled through unwashed skin. The smell of tumored liver in the vicinity of poor Pascal. Creosote, harness soap, tobacco marinated in spit. Bay rum and sweat above Nattie Finn. The odorous assault of Peg Farland's remaining foot. Mold stewed from wet belches and canvas. The callboy touches shoulders and tugs at pant legs. He ducks the slaps and punches that come from the sweltering dark. He darts through all the cars, wrangling the right men for each crew. He pauses long enough to toss his small bundle over Billy Dolph, who sleeps hugging his knees. He leaves Billy alone for now. But he screws the rest—bolters, spikers, gaugers, gandys old and young—to the post of another dollar-and-a-half day.

The Tallow Pot

He sleeps behind Engine No. 212 in the tender car, armored by his stacks of wood like a beetle trapped in amber. He likes it that way. His name is Ode Redfern, and this is his first work train. He started as a yard boy in Nebraska, kept all his digits, lost his wife to typhoid, tried the mines in Colorado, and hated the tunnels. He has more affinity for steam and rail. He finds harmony in the careful tending of a boiler. But building a rail line is slow. Too slow for some. And what good man of the nation doesn't clamor for forwardness and speed?

He's been pushed hard before. There's a story he'll tell over the crackling bowl of his pipe, how he was once the fireman on a narrow-gauge engine near Spearfish Canyon trying to buck snow without a proper plow, just ramming the heavy drifts under orders from a bank man who was in a hurry to get where he was going. They blew too hot, had to shovel the coals right out of the box because the cab was beginning to sizzle and smoke. His engineer, a high-rolling hogger with a reputation for running trestles during gully washes, threw the bank man into the snow with his Gladstone bag. They waited four days before they were towed free. The engineer died a few months later when Elkhorn No. 107 lost air to its brakes and skipped the tracks above Blacktail. He was thrown clear of the engine only to land in a millpond where he was trapped under ice and drowned. This is what keeps Ode Redfern thinking at night, what stacks him in the tender car like a sawed-off length of pine. He can't swim a stroke. He'd rather scald like a skinned rabbit than splash his way to heaven's gates. Worry makes him an attentive fireman.

This morning, like most others, Ode and Joe Hanna, the engineer of No. 212, complain about the paymaster as they fry eggs on a shovel held over the boiler's fire. The cook sells them the eggs at an exorbitant price. They don't dare complain about her.

The Transitman

Is lonely for Chicago. He hasn't perused a city in eight months, hasn't set foot in Illinois for more than a year. He broods as he measures grounds for coffee, ignoring, as he must, Captain Hallock's discussion of his irritable bowels. In Chicago an engineering man can make his fortune. He can erect soaring buildings and defiant bridges that are the darlings of the newspapers hawked on every corner. Patricia writes to him of such marvels. She wishes he were there. Her letters, which no longer tickle the nose with the scent of lavender water once they reach him, are very particular in their desires.

He hears it again—the luff and snap of the canvas that roofs the boarding cars on the work train. It is a constant sound, day and night, now that they are laying track on the naked plains of the Wyoming Territory. The canvas, he has discovered, was manufactured by Thos. A. Moran & Sons, Sailmakers of Chicago. Captain Hallock needles a frequent thread of jokes around this ironical fact. The captain is not above repeating his jokes.

He places his calfskin journal on one knee and licks the nib of his pen as the coffee (sans the eggshell he was unable to procure from the cook) begins to boil. Yesterday, out of exquisite ennui, he wrote about the pomposity of his former teacher, Professor Jules Vanocker. The professor enjoyed quoting Seneca to his mathematics students: "It is better to know useless things than to know nothing at all." Now, as he anticipates his daily performance as second in command of a truculent surveying crew, those words convey the sad blare of an anthem. He believes he knows less than he did when he left Chicago. About himself. About ambition and America.

The surveyors will forge ahead of the work train again this morning. All rod and chain. He will wield the transit. He will read western sunlight through his lenses until his head bursts because there is a problem with the grade along the slope that Caldwell, the draftsman, insists on calling Bosom Hill. It is only half possible this problem will relieve him of his thoughts of Mrs. Baird Gardner. She, too, will leave camp this morning, riding south to the Union Pacific line in Cheyenne, then home to Omaha. Baird Gardner is their topographer, green and eager, a boy who speaks of little other than his wife (whom they have all admired these past six weeks; whom they have all, indeed, overheard in the throes of love).

The transitman never thought he would consider the presence of neckless, mustachioed Mrs. Hallock a blessing, but he does. The sight of Mrs. Hallock quenches a man.

The coffee is brewed. He can already taste it on his embittered tongue, redolent of local alkaloids and the kerosene in which he soaked buffalo chips to make his fire. The eastern sky is bottomless, unfloored, as dizzying in its scope as a bachelor's lust. He etches persistence onto the gilt-edged pages of his journal. He calibrates stoic sentences of the sort his Patricia might wish to read. How there will be no rain today. Only steady calculation and degree. How he will measure the future with length after length of taut, manhandled chain.

The Pounder

He asks to be called Boda, though no one knows whether those brief syllables belong to his first name or his last. He's drawn pay on section gangs since the Union Pacific hawsered itself to Utah in 1869. The palms of his hands are worn down to yellow tendon, but he can still drive a spike, three knocks. And he always wants a baseball game on Sunday, even in a gale. He isn't much for bathing. Donahue says Boda's neck will get its first scrub from the coroner. Boda was, however, the first to offer money for a one-hour lease of Pascal's varnished gramophone. Alas, his delight in music, particularly the melodies of Mr. Stephen Foster, has little apparent influence on the cook, for whom he bears a wordless affection. She isn't a woman for a tune. Yet Boda, who once hung an Idaho card cheat from an upraised wagon tongue because there were no trees nearby, wrings the necks of the dinner fowl when the cook asks him to, and it was he who rescued the Easter ham from the marauding coyote that dragged it off the table during sermon.

The Boomer

Billy Dolph tumbles free of his dreams like a circus aerialist. He's up early, hoping the trick will earn him a chance at two breakfasts, one with each shift. It doesn't. The cook and the pocked girl who's come from a busted claim in the Black Hills to help with the laundry are on to his grin and games. The cook curses the grave of his mother and sends him down the track for curative spices from the Chinese. It'll be his own fault, she says, if Boss Stall sees him and orders him into the hot sun to set spikes. He doffs his cap to Peg Farland, who's doling out picks and shovels from the tool car. When Mr. Hanna, the engineer, plays out his sharp, two-tone whistle for the start of first shift, the rush leaves Billy to barter alone with Old Soo at the Chinese camp. Soo's teeth are as stained as the lip of No. 212's diamond stack. Billy wonders if they got that way from the dog-desperate way Chinamen eat. They pluck slimeys and scaleys from under rocks, that's what Donahue says. Donahue also says Chinese don't wash with soap, but Billy knows that whatever they do or don't do, you never see the yellow bastards yanking at their braids because of lice. He tries not to inhale the steam that curdles above Soo's kettles as he acquires a cigarette paper creased with lumpy brown powder. The price is a dozen peppercorns, two sewing needles, and a worm-free portion of lard. Old Soo pantomimes how the cook should boil the powder in water and pour the hot potion directly onto her aching knuckles.

Billy dodges Boss Stall once more, just long enough to corral Eddie, the callboy. Has Eddie heard about the prospector who hides gold in the crops of his yard geese? The prospector feeds his best nuggets to the birds with their grain. Then he cashes in whenever he wishes, one swing of the ax. And nobody guesses where his gold is hidden. Billy wants Eddie to donate the pyrite he got from that surveyor's wife so they can try the scheme on the cook's chickens. He's sure they'll get the rocks back. Nothing can hurt those birds.

The Editor

Will not make it. He's laid up at the Hotel Niobrara in the soot-and-vinegar town of Newcastle with a scrofular swelling of the testicles. The *Frontier Pioneer Index,* courtesy of the Martineau Brothers of Sandusky, Ohio, will not print an on-track edition to jubilate over this strand of the Great American Steel Web. George, youngest of the ink-stained Martineaus, hopes to placate the railroad's Boston backers by hiring a wagon to haul him and his drawers of lead type north to the frenzy of the corporation's Montana venture instead. He plans to be on his way once the mercury pills have doused his iniquitous fires.

The Goat

Lieutenant Marriner "Peg" Farland lost a leg in Virginia. He was commanding a battery for General A. P. Hill when the Yankees blew splinters of gun carriage and draft horse through his knee. There are whispers that Peg has won and lost fortunes at faro in St. Louis, that he was nearly strung up in Texas. Peg is good with numbers, which means Boss Stall gave him the company store after the Jew absconded for the wonders of the Burlington line. Peg Farland also manages the tool car and is a fair hand over an anvil. This is a blessing since the chief smith, Dot Commiskey, has been slowed by boils.

The complainers gripe that Peg keeps the best tobacco for his own diet, lining his Bollinger hat with quality plugs so they will stay moist in the dry desert air. But none dare accuse him to his face. Peg sports one leg, two swift fists, and the pride of a vanquished officer. He tells the dying Cuban, Pascal, that he is headed for the sparkled waters of San Francisco. Pascal doesn't believe him. Pascal tells Nattie Finn, who tells many others, that Lieutenant Peg Farland of Virginia is meant to live where living is undermined.

Peg Farland is the one who hears the ambush of the chickens.

The Eagle Eye

If only he'd stuck to wiping engine brass or blustering to Ode Redfern about the flanges on the pony truck. But no. The succulent strut of what he believed was a prairie cock was too much. The sight of the bird impaled him with appetite, and he carelessly discharged the gun he keeps mounted in his engine cab. The creature swooned in a mist of blood and feathers only to be identified by Mr. Redfern as one of the cook's mysteriously freed domestics. Thus he, engineer Joseph Hanna, most recently of Fort Pierre, and the quiet Mr. Redfern face a culinary future of boiled mush and recalcitrance. The cook must be placated. She will soon discover who has slaughtered her prize rooster. Redfern claims to know the terrain. He speaks of nearby waters and trout the size of long toms. Joe Hanna asks himself: will the aggrieved cook accept a tribute of fresh fish if he can cajole an efficacious amount of dynamite from Mr. Stall? He is somewhat experienced with dynamite. And the poor luck that has pursued him since the misunderstanding over the bank draft in Ogallala is surely bound to change. How can a gentlemanly gesture go wrong?

The Shack

Brakeman Lafayette Rule is waiting, waiting, waiting in the slim shadow of the crummy car for the overdue supply train to appear. He'd rather eat sparks on a spongy spur line than scratch his ass on a work train, but he's got two brats to feed with another in his wife's belly that may or may not be his own. The five Mormon brothers who teamster fresh ties off the flatcars don't need an extra hand this morning, so Lafayette is whittling a busted ax handle into a new brake club when he hears the uproar. General hue and cry. Like brawling on a Saturday. Lafayette skates down the incline of the roadbed in time to dodge a riderless horse that's headed west, stirrups slapping. He shades his eyes long enough to register that the horse, a bay mare, belongs to Captain Elijah Hallock, surveyor and unskilled equestrian. The mare will soon dig in her heels. She won't care for the blinding miles of unmarked prairie.

Lafayette Rule trots the length of the train. Flatcar, stock car, dining car, washhouse. A whirlwind has descended in the vicinity of the cook's awning. The new laundress, whom Lafayette has already dreamily cast in scenes of unclothed drama, is weeping. The hens are loose and flapping. The cook is beating some young fool with a tent stake amid cries of robbery and murder. The wash cauldron has somehow spilled itself over a prostrate Captain Hallock. The brakeman shoulders through a phalanx of perplexed onlookers until he can assure himself the captain hasn't been poached alongside the week's ration of bedbugs. Someone says the portly captain was pinching sugar when he ran afoul of the cook. A stuttering Swede says n-n-no, the captain was only p-paying his compliments when a loud noise—could it have been a gunshot?—caused his mare to t-toss him into the laundry pot. Someone else says Billy Dolph and the callboy have been caught molesting the chickens.

But that won't be the last word about the misadventure. The tale will have ten verses and a chorus once the rail gangs slaver into it. The boys will lay in hard. They will redouble the humiliations and the mockeries. They will shout them out like sailors. Captain Hallock, in particular, will have to billet with the pagan Chinese if he wants one moment of peace. Lafayette Rule reckons the man might yet wish the laundress's water had been at full boil.

The sound of a whistle susses into his reverie. It's engineer Joe Hanna's signal that the train is moving up. While the least of them have created calumny out of idleness and sport, another mile of singing rail has been laid down like a babe. O creation, thinks Lafayette Rule, as he fingers his vest pocket for the tidy sum he owes the whiskey trader. There will be spirit to spare over the cards tonight. Despite the absence of eggs in the oversalted hash, there will be laughter and roaring in the dark. And how else might a fellow wish to end his day if he must end it in this national wilderness of industry and theft? We are Liberty's living fuse, snorts Lafayette Rule to himself. We are miscreant hands on the Diviner's line.

How Bitter the Weather

I judge their hands. I say to myself, yes, that guy fights fires in the mountains. Or no, that guy's not a roofer, no matter what he claims. Armand has spadelike hands, troweling hands, and they convince me he speaks a certain kind of truth. He woos me with the fused joint of his ring finger, the corrugated grasp of his palms. It seems possible that he quarried rock in the Ausable Valley of New York. He might have loaded shells in a Sherman tank during the war. He tells me he did. It's an undisputed fact he repaired rail for the Union Pacific, working on gangs out of Grand Island and Cheyenne and Ogallala before he retired. He has a card for that, his years on the railroad. He shows it every chance he gets.

I know Armand from the coffee shop, same as everyone else. He keeps a room at the Connor Hotel, paid for with his pension, but he tries to stay out of that room during the day. He drinks when he's there, and he says he knows where the drink will take him. At the coffee shop, he sits at a table by the front windows, sometimes alone with the sports page from the newspaper where I work, sometimes with one of the bank tellers or travel agents from Second Street. They enjoy the heavy vowels of his accent. Armand owns two suits, one of chalk-striped wool. Both suits were tailored for much taller men, but Armand manages to make the pools of extra fabric look dapper. There's always a pressed shirt with cuffs, no tie. His shoes are secondhand cowboy boots, rocker curved from wear. A belted overcoat the color of spilled scotch hangs on the back of his chair and a gray driving cap lies on the table. It's his eyes that define his need and authority—his eyes and those hands. His potent, black gaze has a way of embracing more than I'm prepared for.

Our talk is usually padded and habitual. *Good morning. Is the coffee strong? How is your newspaper? How was your evening rest?* That sort of thing. Armand's short sentences are made longer by his barrel-chested gestures and the ardent sheen of his sun-browned face. When I come through the door of the coffee shop, he some-times leaps to his feet to announce his opinion of the high school sports teams. "*Buon giorno,* Melanie. Those footballers need new kicker, no?" Armand seems to read the *Laramie Daily Boomerang* mostly for its sports coverage, though he's never once been to a game. I haven't been able to convince him that my work as city reporter doesn't make me responsible for the photographs and boxed numbers he admires so much.

We are mere acquaintances, people who stipple one another's lives with greetings and farewells. Armand speaks of his past in anecdotes—smooth stories that I like and am not responsible for. How he comes from generations of stonecutters in northern Italy. How he sailed into New York as a poor man and made a family, as he says, among the upstate Italians only to lose that family, God forgive him. How he went back to Europe with the U.S. Army, where his fel-low GIs taught him to smoke tobacco. He blames them, with laugh-ter, for his stained fingers and teeth. He found work with the U.P. in

Nebraska "when it is time again for the hammer and big skies." He makes no secret of his grief concerning his family. I gather there are children, a forsaken wife of some kind. These facts seem to produce real pain in Armand, and it's this pain that leads him to drink red wine when he's alone with his memories. He tells me he often prays to the Virgin Mother to close his throat against his burning thirst, but she hasn't yet seen fit to grant his prayers. "A bad man," he says to me one morning when the sun is so bright it makes the air near the shop windows smell of flame. "Bad, but the most interesting of men you know. You write about me someday."

I don't give his remarks much thought. I have a job serving up the politics of a small, ambivalent city. I present the issues in sentences that are as cool and mild as sorbet. I won't write about Armand, or any other private citizen, not even in my journal.

This is how I feel before Armand disappears.

I hear about it from Tommy, one of the college kids who has learned to brew decent espresso. Tommy likes Armand and keeps the rude boy patrons from making fun of his accent and the way he cadges day-old muffins. Tommy and Armand pass the time swapping opinions on world affairs. Armand once got so worked up about socialism that Germaine, the owner of the coffee shop, asked him to step outside and walk it off. "We joke about him being in here so much," Tommy says. "How like if he doesn't show up, I'll know he's dead or sick, so I worried the first day, decided to check on him except we were busy and I didn't get it done right away. Then I remembered what he said last week about a sister in Denver, so I chilled."

"A sister?" I've come to the counter for lemon peel. Tommy tends to skimp on lemon peel.

"Yeah." Tommy shrugs under the sleeveless shirt that airs his deltoids. "He said something about going to see her. Taking the bus to Colorado."

It makes sense. Thanksgiving is coming up; it's time to tangle the family knots. I go back to my table. There's no reason to call my friend Cole, the policeman, or the hospital.

"I did dial his place one time," Tommy says. "Phone number he gave me. No answer. Should I keep trying?"

"Probably not," I say. "Armand should visit wherever he wants."

Then Cinda, who comes on shift at eleven, re-spins the whole wheel for us. "He talked about being sick, how it made him think of this kind of soup his mother made for him when he was young, and how he wanted to have that soup again. He has an ulcer maybe." Cinda is long limbed and elegantly bracketed by the cluster of Chinese characters tattooed at the nape of her neck. Armand sometimes celebrates her loveliness by serenading her sotto voce during lunch. I know from experience that Cinda enjoys elaborating her charms for men and women alike. "Anyway, I heated him some broth Germaine was saving for stock and he appreciated that. I'm not good at listening to medical stuff. I might have missed something. But Armand, well, you know, when the two of us talk it's mostly about being a Gypsy."

I look into Cinda's kohl-rimmed eyes while I dig in my canvas pack for a notepad just like I would for a real news story. I find the gold-leaf flecks in those eyes, and the footloose longing. Tommy, who is rinsing coffee filters, asks her to say it again.

"God, Tommy, you know what I mean. Armand's a Gypsy, like his whole family is, from Romania and all those countries. I know he told Melanie about it. He *likes* her."

I shake my head, noting the signal flare of jealousy.

"He got caught in the world war. It's terrible how he tells it, what he can remember from being so young. They got rounded up, right, just like the Jews. Robbed and put on trains and some killed and some sent to those camps, the concentration ones. He has the tattoo for it. On his arm. Didn't he ever show you?"

I shake my head again. So does Tommy. Neither of us has ever seen more than Armand's burly wrists. He never rolls up his cuffs.

"But he talks Italian," Tommy says. "We did Mussolini, Garibaldi, the whole thing. So how's he do that? Italian and Romanian?"

Cinda bears down. "Gypsies transcend borders. That's why everybody hates them and they're so despised by history. Armand speaks a lot of languages. He's way better educated than us Americans."

I ask, "Did he say anything about a sister?"

"No." She runs blunt fingernails through her spritzy hair. "His whole family was killed in the war."

The pieces of this story don't add up. I think about satisfaction and its elusiveness, then I tell Cinda and Tommy I'll get in touch with the sister, if there is one, to make sure Armand's okay. Cinda slips a piece of banana bread into my pack. It's the kind of offering I've come to expect from her: dry and mute. I pull on my watch cap, my mittens, yank my mountain bike out of the stand that's in front of the shop. I can't see Medicine Bow Peak because of low clouds and a fine, cold rain, but I'm looking for it anyway when a sixty-car coal train from the Powder River Basin tears through the rail yard across the street. The empty sidewalk shudders under my feet. Armand loves this sight, his yellow-nosed trains piercing the pretend fabric of the town. I watch the engine wheels lash the rainwater into steam. No matter what I've told Cinda and Tommy, it's time to bring Cole into things.

We meet on Third Street, hunched like weary parishioners beneath the drizzle. The Connor Hotel was once a cattlemen's haven, then a flophouse. Now it's a reasonably clean honeycomb of apartments for single working people. Cole says we'll just knock on the door. There's no cause—yet—to do more. He knows I've called the hospital, the downtown clinic, and the VA in Cheyenne, though I now have reason to wonder whether Armand's really a veteran of any war. I told Cole this when I called him at the station.

The pale second-story walls smell of a hundred years of

transience, all breath and restlessness. There's no answer at the brown door of Number 23, no answer at the neighbor's either, though we disturb several cats. How long has it been? Two days? Three? Cole makes up his mind. He knocks harder on Armand's door, then puts his weight against it. It isn't locked. We're met by a slab of dry, neglected air, nothing more.

We're both relieved. People in Wyoming get isolated, and they tend to . . . well, it's easier on everyone if a man disposes of himself outdoors. A man should *take* responsibility, that's one of Cole's beliefs. Standing in that tiny room, shielded by his broad, competent back, I know what Cole is saying to himself. He's saying, *That's how I'll go when I have to, I'll just goddamn disappear.*

I ask if we can look for the sister's phone number, or a note. We can't assume he's dead, can we? Or safe in Denver. We're his friends. . . .

But that's a false claim. I'm not a real friend. I haven't done shit for Armand except humor his rants and pantomimed jokes.

We search with sweeping eyes and fingers. Cole finds a few prescription bottles in the bathroom. One of the medications is for high blood pressure. We don't recognize the others. Cole gets the name of a local doctor—an internist—off a label. The chives in the refrigerator are still fresh; the milk isn't. The shallow closet holds four starched shirts wrapped in plastic from the cleaner's and Armand's lightweight summer suit. There are pillars of hats stacked on a high, unpainted shelf. Panamas, peaked caps, homburgs, berets—all brushed and cared for. Most of them still have their tags. Since we've never seen Armand in anything other than his overcoat and driving cap—no matter how bitter the weather—we accept the hats as a private passion, the kind of attic indulgence we all deserve.

Cole says it's barely permissible for him to go through the suitcase and cardboard box. We find them under the twin bed with its pigeon's view of the alley. I hope they contain some answers, the kind of hodgepodge trail guide most of us keep under our beds, or keep somewhere, to prove we've actually worn a path across time and this big country. No dice. There aren't any bank statements, citations, bills, or receipts, no documentation of any kind except materials from the railroad union. The box holds a few magazines and the accordion folds of recent newspaper clippings that don't seem linked by subject or place. Some of them mention tornadoes. The suitcase is better. In it Cole finds library cards from counties all over Wyoming and Nebraska. We find a cheap tin pennywhistle, the kind my father knew how to play. And the scrapbook. That's what I call it. Cole says it's a folder because the photographs—eleven in all—are just stacked inside, not organized or displayed. It doesn't matter. It's all of Armand's family we'll ever get.

Cole radios in a lunch break, and I take him back to my house on Eleventh Street. It's an old place, framed with timber salvaged from Fort Sanders when it was abandoned by the cavalry in the 1880s. It's narrow, crooked, remarkable mostly because of its lousy basement. I love it. Cole loves it when he wants to get laid in the middle of the day. He often talks about the small foothills ranch he hopes to buy when he's able.

I make a pot of tea and shut my tabby cat upstairs, hoping I can gain access to Cole's clear, nonbossy thinking. We've known each other since we were kids, and for three years we had an exclusive relationship, a comfort tour of softball and sex and camping in the mountains. But Cole wants a big house out of town and a child, maybe two, before he's thirty-five. He believes you avoid complications by staying uncomplicated. We called it off, both of us, and I'm still careful about seeing him at the station or the courthouse. He's been a cop for the city almost as long as I've been a reporter.

Cole gives a patient account of what the state police will want to know about Armand and how he'll get word to the regional hospitals. He speculates about what Armand's doctor might say. Yet everything about him—the tilt of his head, the addition of sugar

to his black tea—counsels me to let go of the search. There are
crescent bruises under Cole's hazel eyes. They've been there since a
gay man was pistol-whipped to death on the prairie outside town.
Cole's hard work in the city has become harder, but he still believes
an answer will come to me, to us, as we assemble the facts. We
don't have to chase anything.

Cole doesn't appreciate the sustenance of questions like I do.
He's not a curious guy. He doesn't know about my married lover,
the Episcopal priest, and he doesn't know about the diet pills I like
a little too much. He knows a lot, Cole does—about my sister, the
veterinarian, and the parents retired to Flagstaff—but there's not
much more he can learn about me with that information.

I ask, "Has Armand been causing trouble?"

Besides drinking, Cole says, there's a harassment problem
with a waitress at the Rancher. She got fed up and made a com-
plaint. And there's some sort of loitering thing outside homes on
Ivinson Street. He's not so clear on that one. Armand is lonely or
losing it is what he figures. Same coin, two sides.

I think about the gray bungalow on Ivinson Street, the story
Armand told me about the tanner's wife who lived there once, how
she wasted away during a winter spent staring toward her childhood
home in the east. Her spirit still haunts the front yard, according to
Armand. He collects things like that, local tales of trickery and grief.

I ask, "What about the photographs?"

Cole says I'm the reporter, not him. I've got a studio name on
the back of the portraits and an address in Pennsylvania. He bets I
can date the photos from the style of clothes the woman is wearing
and the chairs the kids are sitting on.

I say, "Nineteen twenties or just before." The woman's mauve
eyes are ageless, without much personality. Something deprived is
sealed in the time capsule of her untinted face. But the children are
transformed like daylilies from one picture to the next. Gowns to
knickers to long pants and all that. Their cheeks and chins are round

with pride. Maybe I'm wrong about the date. Nineteen twenty is much too early for Armand's New York wife and family. Or is it?

Cole knows how much I crave the centrifugal force of orgasm when I'm stuck on a story. We leave the kitchen for the convenience of my dining-room rug. Cole maintains his athlete's body—we first screwed on the bench seat of a high school van when we were both playing soccer—and he expects me to be ready for his haste. He's tongue and insistence; I'm the urgent grip. It's nothing like being with the priest, the flung-high burdens of hesitation and guilt that shadow us like watchtowers and make each kiss burn like a brand. Cole is decent, unfettered. We haven't gotten far enough into the dining room to close the drapes, so the windows are open to a slow, spinning snowfall and the black outreach of the cottonwood trees on my lawn. I wonder when I'll need, or want, to stop fucking Cole. He's still my most bearable complication.

I make him stay on the floor with me, on the lanolin scour of the rug, until our skin begins to buckle in the cold. The water stain at the base of my brass chandelier is the same color as the children's eyes in Armand's nested photographs. I ask Cole why we didn't find any wine bottles—full or empty—in the apartment. He says some drunks are picky, trying to keep secrets even from themselves. The bottles are probably in his neighbor's trash. "Armand's funny," he says, rolling onto a hip to shake out his creased blue pants. I rest my palm at the base of his spine, hoping he's sleeping with someone else he likes, but knowing he's not. Cole says, "With me it's always baseball, what Armand wants to talk about. The Rockies, the Giants, the boys in American Legion. I don't know why. I'm not that big a fan. It's just what he decided we had to have in common."

That night I lie awake, waiting. It's the wrong thing to do. I should be reading or working my contacts on the city council, getting a feel for the upcoming vote on zoning. They never come if you wait for them. But I feel thin. I'm sleepless, undone by a weird blend of skepticism and hope, and I'd like to see my ghost.

I knew the house had a reputation when I bought it. Previous owners had encounters with cavalrymen: soldiers playing cards in the parlor, men loitering in the front hall, the harsh smell of pipe tobacco above the empty stairs. But I see something else. Twice he's come late in the night on a platter of still, cold air. No wind. No lost scents or perfumes. The first time he was motionless, and I was surprised by the silence more than anything. He was so solid, so substantial, I waited for the creak of his boots. He was outfitted for the trenches of World War I with a tin-pot helmet, flapped pockets, gas mask, canteens, a leather-strapped pack. His face was empty of everything but the congealed pallor of fatigue. When he disappeared, taken from my eyes like an image spliced out of a film, I felt dizzy, as if I'd been under the surface of a lake for too long. I got out of bed and touched the floor where he'd stood. Then I looked onto the moon-patched quilt of my front yard. There was nothing to find.

The second visit was different. He wore an ill-fitting blue robe and pajamas. He seemed to be in a hospital, though I couldn't see any bandages. I saw his face more clearly that time, the square hairline and small, upturned nose of a Norwegian or a Swede. He was a big man and younger than I remembered, almost too young to shave his chin. He watched me carefully, for what felt like a long time. There was the glaze of liniment or something medicinal on his forehead, and his eyes were a faded, surrendering gray. He looked colonized to me, too far from home. Then he began to gesture with his clean, bony hands. I understood he was asking me a question, but I didn't hear anything except the buffeting leaps of my cat; she was stalking something in the kitchen downstairs. I've waited ever since—it's been more than two months—for him to come back and ask his question again.

I've told a few people about the ghost. I'm not worried about exorcising him with a little talk. If that were possible, my house and my town and this entire frontier state would be as blanched and unhaunted as a space station. And they aren't. There's plenty of haunting around here. Denial never banishes history or loss, I know that. So I talk about the ghost sometimes, though not to lovers who are too skittish as it is. I told Armand. It was the same afternoon Armand told me about the giant who lived in his parents' village in the Val di Zoldi, a true giant—more than seven feet tall—clad in the skins of mountain wolves. According to Armand, this giant was generous to everyone but the soldiers of the ruling duke. He gave Armand's mother a length of red Chinese silk and a silver button in exchange for a meal, though the button was later torn from his mother's bodice by a greedy church bishop. We were in the coffee shop, and Armand teased me a little. He suggested I was entertaining nothing more in my bedroom than a despised, unclaimed soldier of the duke.

"But what if that's not it?" I said, feeling suddenly light boned, threaded by a single idea. "What if he thinks *he* should be there—in the house—instead of me?"

"Melanie, *mia* Melanie." Armand compressed his lips until they disappeared. "You live a life of loves and waiting because that is your want. This does not mean it is a wanting for the whole world."

Loves and waiting? Was sneaky Armand suggesting he knew about my married boyfriend? Or was he telling me who he thought I really was? The intrusion bothered me. "That's not what I'm saying, Armand. Mister Soldier Ghost can be wherever he wants to be. I don't mind him in the house. I'm willing—hell, I'm happy—to share my space."

Armand pinched at the handle of his coffee mug. I'd seen the motion before when he worried the black strand of his rosary. "Is not about space," he said contritely. "That someday you understand."

Maybe this is why I want the ghost now. I've been thinking of Armand, taking notes, making more calls. I've confirmed he doesn't have a working phone line in his apartment. He doesn't have an account with the phone company, never has. I wonder who Tommy called that day and why Armand gave him a phone number at all. Cole has no news. The doctor wouldn't say anything specific about Armand's health, though he agreed that an older man in Armand's "condition" might get depressed. "What's his condition?" I asked Cole. "What's that bullshit mean?" I think back to when Armand and I talked, sliding sentences across the cafe table like cards. We made jokes about my soldier ghost showing up for the wrong war. We laughed. I left Armand and went into an afternoon braceleted by high, white clouds. They were spaced like beads on an invisible string.

People here have known me all my life, since my father's days as the downtown pharmacist. They think I took the job at the *Boomerang* because it's what I could get after college, being smart but not smart in the sciences like my sister, who has a thriving small animal practice in Colorado. You aren't supposed to strive in Wyoming. You take what's available. That's how we do it here. I try to see it another way. That I have a job—maybe even a purpose—that lets me patrol this pioneer place I love and don't love. I was born before the last big boom so I've seen my hometown crown itself with great plans, then dwindle. Laramie: a city awry, shredded like a prayer flag by the constant gusting wind.

Before midnight, I call in a favor from a high school friend. He's not asleep either, and he's not surprised to hear from me. He was an electrician in the Green River mines until he took a cut in pay to work for the railroad closer to home. He says I should get to the U.P. shop early and ask for him or T.W., the steward. They'll tell me what they can.

I walk to the far side of town when the horizon is still iron plated with darkness. The viaduct over the rail yard is black and burning cold to the touch. You can see the whole city from up there, cloaked in the purple vapor of weak streetlights—the slattern houses near the tie yard, the sandstone imposition of the Episcopal cathedral where my lover is doubtless on his knees in predawn prayer, the repainted face of First Street, so often made over, so nervous about rejection. This morning there's a girl standing on the far end of the viaduct, leaning into the hot rush of a freight train on its way south to Denver. I pass behind her. She's wearing red shoes and some man's tentacled jacket. I know she's thought of jumping, but she won't. We don't kill ourselves under the willful gaze of our town.

An hour later I'm buying an espresso from Tommy. We commiserate by avoiding one another's eyes. I think about how to tell Tommy what I heard at the rail yard. They haven't seen Armand in days. They're not too cut up about his absence because he hangs around there a lot, him and his opinions, asking questions about the pension and all that, wanting the guys to vote on every little thing. Plus, he hasn't been so welcome since the incident with Bud Kobalarski and the glass windows on his front porch. T.W., the steward, is thinking of clearing out all the old farts who sit in chairs near the back door to his office, though it'll be hard on some of them, especially Jerry Mahan, who's been around since the brick roundhouse was torn down in 1976. This is what I hear from my electrician friend, Sammy Vialpando, who's got a new house on Kearney Street and a baby on the way. I heard it, and I walked back across the viaduct toward a dawn that smelled of rust and the sluggish, shouldering river. The girl in the jacket was gone. Did you like Armand? I asked Sammy, talking loud enough for him to hear through the pink earplugs he wears to muffle the stamp of the mill. He put on his leather gloves. "You say hello to a man every day don't mean you make him your business. Strange old dude. Lot of them are strange to me. I got a good job here. I'm working."

Tommy brings me my tiny, burnt-smelling drink just after

I dry swallow one of my pick-me-up pills. The woman who owns the pottery studio above the bank comes into the coffee shop. She has the look: mouth half open and rounded with a greeting for Armand. But there's no Armand here to reflect our habits. Sorry, Tommy tells me, nobody has a single piece of news and Germaine is very worried. So is he. Also, somebody's been in looking for me, a person named Gail from the soup kitchen that operates out of the basement of the Episcopal cathedral. It wasn't about Armand, though, Tommy says, what this person Gail wanted to tell me. The needle stab of a secret in collapse runs from my throat to my belly. Gail from the church. I try to bring her face to mind—surely it's a shallow and dented face, and surely she's got an opinion about women who tempt good Christian men—but I can't picture her, even though I've volunteered at the soup kitchen many times.

Armand used to eat lunch there. It's also where I met my priest, where I scrubbed shriveled vegetables donated by local grocers and eventually lifted a cassock for a quiet blow job. Armand would say to me, he'd say, "Melanie, always working. Never the fun." Then he'd grin around the brown spindles of his teeth, old men on either side of him snuffling soup. Melanie. Never the fun. And my jaw aches with fatigue. And I need to walk the long, frigid mile back to my house while it's still early enough to hear the bark of confined dogs. I haven't learned enough yet. Will I ever learn enough?

Cole phones me at the *Boomerang*. What he says drives me outside, where I stand under a blue pavilion of sky so seamless it makes my eyes burn. The sheriff's office has gotten a call. "You're ready for this, right? We talked about it. You know what they'll find." Cole uses his uninflected cop's voice. Yes, I know. I live here, where we think we've kept the worst of the world at bay with cold weather and poor soil. The Arapaho knew better than to stay in these foothills once winter came. But the white people stayed, and I've stayed, and I'm the sorry scavenger of more than words. "It's okay, Mel," Cole says. "Armand did what he had to do." It's not okay. I cross the street to the steps of Saint Laurence's, the Catholic church built by the long-gone Irish. Armand goes to mass here once or twice a week, right across from my office. My town looks alive from these steps, laden and gritty. I sit. I try not to think because thinking only brings more questions, and I'm already a woman bricked over by questions. What will the sheriff find in the erosion and pit of that canyon? Rags? Bone fragments of shame? Importance?

We often find the emptied bodies of men at the edges of our town, old men and young men like the one who was murdered. We don't handle outsiders very well. I'm trying to decide if this is our final frontier.

So, here's Armand—not the last time I saw him because I can't think about the last time. I was on these steps. He was walking up Grand Avenue in his unbuttoned coat, his bull neck bowed as if he'd just hoisted a load. The afternoon was burnished with sunlight and the frail gold of windblown pollen. Armand looked like a stonecutter for once, heir to a long line of laborers despite his heeled boots and pinstripes. Why *was* he here? I'd asked him that a dozen times. He said he liked the town, the friendly people, and the always fresh air, who would not? He ambled past the barbershop and the title company. Past the tobacco store and the dry hedge in front of the *Boomerang* office. I didn't call out. I didn't gesture for him to join me and the plain turkey sandwich I was having for lunch. But he saw me and gave a semaphore wave with both arms before he crossed the gray street. Then he stood below on the sidewalk, reading me as though I were a worn bronze plaque anchored to the church wall. The sparrows hoping for a handout rose between us on their scraps of wing, and his black eyes were so expectant I turned to see if the carved doors to the sanctuary had swung open.

"You are wrong in what you want." This is what he said to me.

He said he knew me and he knew my haunted house, though he'd never been inside. It's true. I never invited Armand anywhere. But he'd seen my home, walked by it many times day and night just as he walked by the newspaper office and the coffee shop and over the viaduct to the neighborhoods of industry and neglect where the railroad still breathed fire. He saw us inhabiting land that was once uninhabitable. He saw the sharp ricochet of strangers. And he knew what he believed in. Our hearts. My failing performance as a bad girl. The trains of America passing us by. "That ghost you see, he is not asking your help or help from anybody. He is done asking. He is in that place of your room maybe, and you are in that place at the same minute, and that is all can be said of the soldier ghost. You look too much, Melanie, and you do not see. He comes . . . he goes, your ghost. Wound or no wound. He is in the world of people who care. No difference than you or than me."

That was what he told me. He sat while I finished my sandwich, then he levered his sore joints to stand and go into his chapel. A nap out of the hot sun, he said. Or a few moments of prayer, whatever he and the Blessed Mother agreed on. I smelled the flat starch of his shirt and the invisible fruit of wine. I smelled the leakage of his sighs. I asked how long he would stay. He opened the heavy wooden doors of the church, and he closed them without giving me an answer, leaving me with the local sparrows gathered at my feet for their regular diet of crumbs.

Superstitions of the Indians

It started with the grant money. You know the drill. You're finishing a PhD in consumer textile design or medieval philology or comparative cultural studies (like me), but you don't get the comfy fellowship from the X Foundation; that fellowship goes to a whiz kid working in what nice people call "the extractive industries." You still need to finance your research. You've been on campus many long, lean years. You've outlasted two advisors, both of whom have moved on to towns with better football teams and restaurants. Faculty skeptics arch their eyebrows whenever they see you anyplace other than the library.

It's time to step up to the plate, get untracked, give 110 percent.

Otherwise, you'll end your days dusting the spines of Italian cookbooks at Barnes & Noble.

So I applied for, and won, a grant from the university's

American Heritage Archives—the AHA! as it's known to campus wags (like me). The grant was three thousand dollars for the summer, just enough to finance both my research and my defense of the citywide Frisbee golf title. The problem was the grant required me to work in the Bedard Collection of the archives, a moldering selection of books and maps gathered by the late Grace Frances Bedard, former reservation schoolteacher, former university librarian, original old bat. Though I hadn't said so in my application, there wasn't a single document in the Bedard Collection I really wanted to look at. It didn't matter. I had to play the game to earn the check.

I took the high road. I got out of bed at 9:00 a.m. on the first Monday in June and ate some mango-flavored yogurt. I asked my girlfriend, Sukie (a student in geographic information sciences), if we could schedule the strenuous sex at her place for a while. Then I stretched and took a two-hour ride on the dual-suspension mountain bike I had bought from a guy in environmental law. By 1:00 p.m. I was showered, if not shaved, and ready to meet the chief archivist of the AHA.

Holly-Carol Nyquist was tall and frosty lipped, and she knew a wanker when she saw one. She was pure Old Guard—an abbess in her cloister, a paper-sniffing priestess who still mourned the loss of card catalogs. As she examined me from beneath a Valkyrie visor of graying bangs, she asked pointed questions about my dissertation. I lied like an untenured professor. Yes, I had done a thorough search of the relevant databases. Yes, I understood the unique and subtle significance of the underutilized Bedard Collection. No, I would not burden her hardworking staff with ignorant questions. Holly-Carol Nyquist wasn't fooled, but she signed my request forms nonetheless. Then she produced a smile, a chilly grimace made perverse by the lascivious gap between her front teeth. I had no idea what the hell I was in for—that's what the smile conveyed. It gave me the creeps.

Ms. Nyquist passed me along to R. W. S. Bassingdale, senior archivist, for a formal orientation. But Mr. Bassingdale was overwhelmed by the task of trying to mount salmon flies from a big donor's fly-fishing collection in time for a fund-raising brunch, so he punted me to young Lacy Proffit, a recovering science librarian who worked the desk in the secluded G. F. Bedard Memorial Reading Room. Lacy Proffit, a zaftig brunette carefully packed into a pair of black capri pants, was on her headset phone. She waved to me, she rolled her hazel eyes, she sashayed between her chair and the cubbyholes where researchers stashed their backpacks and briefcases. "Hollywood," she finally whispered, pointing to her headset. "Some guy wants to fly out here just so he can *touch* Barbara Stanwyck's Oscar statuette, the one she got as an honorary award in the eighties. He's a little obsessed. I'm trying to cool his jets. Why don't you get started."

The Solitary Scholar at last! The very thought made my feet itch.

I did have a plan. Charlie Plantar, a guy two years ahead of me, had just landed a tenure-track job on the East Coast. Charlie's dissertation analyzed the iconography of steam engines in the American West. If trains were job-market hip today, the smart money said they would be passé tomorrow—but not too passé. Transportation theory would retain its traction for at least one more employment cycle. I loved bikes. And I knew a lot about them. The AHA had a garage-sized collection of nineteenth-century cycling materials—manuals, photographs, ad campaigns, the works. But I couldn't investigate them right away. I had to do my penance in the Bedard Collection first.

I dozed over a stack of abstracts for nearly an hour. The reading room was stuffy and empty. I couldn't even distract myself by launching spitballs at other academic ants. Lacy Proffit was still on the telephone, though the conversation had evidently moved well beyond Barbara Stanwyck. There'd been laughter on Lacy's end, then giggling, then something I recognized as estrogen-fueled breathlessness. I was glad when Lacy saw fit to take her California call through the doorway marked STAFF ONLY. I feared for the seams of her capri pants. She returned about ten minutes later, face flushed, lips swollen, the phone headset clenched around her neck like one of Cleopatra's golden collars. She was humming the theme song to *Big Valley*.

I caught her glassy hazel eye. "Hollywood?" I asked. "Did you talk Mr. Hot Jets out of, er, coming?"

"No!" she squeaked. "I mean, yes. I—he wants to know more! But I—"

"It's okay. I've got what I need today. That's if you don't mind me going into the stacks alone." This was against policy, but I wasn't above taking advantage of Lacy Proffit's oxygen-deprived state.

"I don't mind," Lacy said, her cheeks mottled with passion. "You seem like a good guy."

The Good Guy wanted more than anything to saunter through the trash heap of the Bedard Collection, pull a few books, pile them on a table, then find a computer terminal where he could do some real work. Leaving Lacy Proffit to her vasodilation, I stepped over the velvet rope that kept the riffraff away from Grace Bedard's pack-rat obsessions. I paused briefly at the wall of railroad monographs that had launched Charlie Plantar toward prosperity, then followed the stink of new glue, old calfskin, and nervous sweat into the shadows, hoping against hope that someone had wired a computer somewhere in that dark maze.

No such luck. The deeper I went into the claustrophobic stacks, the less organized or even recognizable the collection became. Books were crammed horizontally onto shelves. Their spines were untagged and unnumbered. What looked like bales of old newspaper spilled onto the floor in some places, and I wondered if anyone had walked the aisles that week, or even that month. The linoleum tile was whiskered with dust. It was depressing. All that information, all those memories and intentions—and no one was interested. Least of all me. Grace Bedard had labored long and hard in Wyoming mining camps and Indian schools before she became the university's first librarian. She'd probably never even seen a bicycle.

I checked my digital triathlon watch. Ten minutes until closing. I started to imagine how cool it would be to Frisbee a route through the low-ceilinged AHA. As I calculated the trajectories and spin, I began to think of Sukie, who was a kick-ass Ultimate player. Thinking of Sukie redirected my blood flow as Sukie's other major talent was kicking my ass in bed. You can see how it happened, right? How a charismatic Man of Letters might trip over a warped floor tile, thrown off balance by the woody inspired by his Muse? I slammed into the nearest overstuffed shelf. The book came straight for me, out of the gloom like a comet bound for earth. It bounced off my intelligent forehead, made my ears ring like cymbals, filled my nose with an explosion of nasty-smelling dust. Then it fell at my feet. "Ouch," I whimpered, overcome with pain and sneezing. "That hurt."

"Yes, indeedy." Lacy Proffit's sated voice eased through the ache between my watering eyes. "Time to close up shop."

"Uh, yeah. All right," I replied, surprised anyone could hear me. I felt as though I was miles from the beehive activity of the AHA, as if the actual landscape had shifted under my feet. Trying not to sniffle, I lifted the book from where it rested across the toes of my running shoes. It was a heavy volume (which I already knew), squat, rebound in the bright yellow cloth usually reserved for children's books. No title. The endpapers were nicely marbled. I noticed them before I crammed the infernal thing into the nearest available shelf space, not far from where it had fallen.

I stumbled back to the world of velvet ropes and capri pants, wiping my bruised noggin on a sleeve. The day was about to improve. The weather was awesome, and I had a disc golf match scheduled against a trio of overconfident Sigma Nus. We were going to play the way I liked to play—for money.

The next morning I was sick. Sukie noticed it as she was straddling me. I confess: I was so smothered by my strange dream about Frisbees that morphed into thumping drumheads, I didn't even know we were doing it. Sukie could tell I was off. "You're hot," she said, feeling my forehead while she shimmied. "I think you've got a fever."

"I don't feel so good," I croaked, noting my fatigue and what felt like a serious sore throat. "I mean, except for what you're doing."

"Well, yeah, a virus isn't going to stop that. In fact, orgasm is probably good for you." She grinned. "Purifying."

I didn't feel very pure, not at all, but I never liked to let Sukie down. She counted on me for my vigor. She was very clear about that. It was the one thing that kept me ahead of the more ambitious lads in her PhD program. I lay back and thought of gear ratios until she was done.

"I'll fix you some tea before I leave," she said, flexing her wonderful hamstrings over the heap made by the sheets and my body. "Do you think you can take Nico out?" Nico was her arthritic Alsatian.

I nodded, unwilling to torture my inflamed throat with words.

"Maybe you should walk him up to student health. They're not busy in the morning, and they give away awesome drugs. You look terrible."

"Thanks."

Sukie leaned over and kissed the bruise between my eyes. Strangely, her hair smelled of wood smoke. "Cute, but terrible. Take advantage of the free health care while you can."

After Sukie left for her lab, I somehow tore myself away from her queen-sized futon and stumbled into the shower. The cold water was more help than the honey oatmeal shampoo or the lemon aloe body wash. The cold water confirmed I was alive. I dressed, combed my hair, forced myself to choke down the bitter swill Sukie had left steeping on the kitchen counter. Nico, whose breath bore hints of all the carrion he'd scarfed in better days, waited for me by the door, a red leash dangling from his worn teeth. "All right, you gee-zer," I said, noting the urine that had started to leak down his hind leg. "I give in. We're going to the doc."

Six blocks on a summer day, and it was all I could take. My stomach was steady, but the rest of me felt cored out, burned to a crisp, swimming with poison. I tied Nico to a bench outside the student health center so he could suffer the fat and arrogant pa-rade of campus squirrels. I was ushered right in to see a doctor.

Dr. Illium, that's what the name tag said. He was a young guy, not much older than I was—probably not any older, if I really thought about it. Clean-cut except for a sad soul patch beneath his lower lip. He wore blue scrubs, a stethoscope, and a pair of scuffed brown clogs. Why do all the hip physicians wear clogs? I wanted to ask Dr. Illium that, but he got to his questions first.

"Where'd you get the bruise?" He pointed at my brow.

"Aggressive reference material," I said, hoping a sore throat wouldn't undermine my sardonic delivery. "Professional hazard. You know what it's like."

He nodded. "With me, it's slip-and-fall sputum. Gets me every time. Put your ass on that table."

Dr. Illium listened to me meander through my incredibly basic symptoms. He didn't seem impressed until he began to prod my throat with one of those wide, splintery Popsicle sticks. "Hunhhh," he said, tugging at my lips with his dry fingers. "Hmmmm. Errrraaahyep." He asked me to swallow. He asked me about strep, staph, tonsillitis, gonorrhea, HIV. I told him I was as healthy as a diet of tuna crackers and Mountain Dew allowed.

"You've got some impressive eruptions in there." Dr. Illium gestured toward my throat as if it were a traveling art exhibit. "I'd like to swab them, see what we can grow."

"You think it's bacterial?" Just saying a word with that many syllables brought on fresh needles of pain.

"I don't know what I think. Things in there are . . . a little unusual. Did you say you were in the military?"

I had said no such thing. The question increased the clamminess of my sweat.

"How about vaccinations? Did your parents keep everything up to date?"

I nodded. "What are you saying, Doc? Is this more than a go-home, suck-on-an aspirin kind of gig? Am I infected?"

"Don't know." Dr. Illium produced an unconvincing shrug. "I doubt it. But I did a brief stint in the Middle East, saw a few GIs with throats like yours. It's just . . . unusual."

"How worried should I be?"

"Not at all until I tell you different. I'd like to load you up with analgesics and throat lozenges. And I want you to promise you'll spend the next twenty-four hours in bed."

I thought of the twenty-mile bike ride I had planned, my dissertation, Sukie's evening softball game. All that responsibility made me crave a supersized nap. "In bed," I whispered. "And you'll call me about the swab."

"I'll call. Or I'll have you quarantined." Dr. Illium gave me a very naughty wink.

Nico and I tottered back to Sukie's place, where I filled his bowl with fresh water and put Radiohead on the CD player. I hadn't even pulled up the sheets before I was dreaming again. It was horses, this time. Pitiful, starving horses streaked and spotted with what looked like bright finger paint. They had no riders. I slept to the slow, doomed sound of their hooves for hours.

When I woke up, I found Nico snoring into one of my armpits. I felt a little better but still too lousy to handle a bike ride. Despite my promise to Dr. Illium, I didn't plan to waste the whole day. The only thing I was fit for was a brief, obsequious visit to the AHA. Sukie had been back to check on me—there was a note on the kitchen counter underneath what looked like a wad of moldy rubber bands. *Drink me,* the note said, fortune-cookie style, *so you can be the satisfy.* I put the green wad in my front pocket.

Normally, I could have run from Sukie's to the AHA in five easy minutes. This was not a normal day. I sucked on the nasty, numbing lozenges just to keep my throat open, and my eyes were so photosensitive I had to wear both my sunglasses and my Detroit Pistons cap. By the time I got to the crosswalk in front of the AHA, I felt like I'd traversed the Sinai with Lawrence of Arabia. I didn't even have enough bone in my spine to ride the elevator four floors to the Bedard Collection. My only hope was the lounge. I could recover from my dizziness in the lounge. Gather my strength. Otherwise, the day would be a total loss.

I'd been in the lounge a few times, most recently for a fellow student's Christian poetry slam. It was a neutral square equipped with small tables, a sink, a microwave, and packets of sugar pilfered from McDonald's. Two people were at the tables when I staggered in, a bearded latte drinker in chinos and an older lady reading from a thick hardcover book. I managed to fill my mug with water and stick it in the microwave before I collapsed. My balance was gone. My hearing was warped. I felt like I was sealed in a tunnel of sloshing dishwater.

The chinos man left before the microwave beeped. I was wondering how the hell I was going to stand up to retrieve my mug when I felt an island of cool temperature float across my shoulders. It was a human hand. The hand belonged to the old lady I'd seen engrossed in her book.

"Might I be permitted to help?" she asked.

"No, thanks," I said, enjoying the cool comfort that spread deliciously between my scapulae. "Just getting my act together. I'm a little tired, that's all."

The old lady stared at me through both levels of her bifocals. "Young man," she said, and I could tell she was struggling to maintain her patience, "you are clearly more than tired. Feverish, I'd say. Thoughtlessly contagious. And on the verge of delirium. At least allow me to prepare your beverage."

I shrugged. She was an insistent old bird. I pulled Sukie's herbal wad from my pocket. "Could you use this?" I asked. My words surprised me. I didn't recall sending them to my mouth.

The old lady gently removed the herb ball from between my shaking fingers. She scrutinized it through her glasses, sniffed it with rabbity nostrils, then popped it into her open mouth. "Certainly," she muffled. "A very wise choice, if somewhat makeshift." She spat out the wad. It lay like a giant goober in her palm. "But you need additional aid, if you don't mind a friend's suggestion." She pointed to a much-folded square of paper that had somehow appeared on the table in front of me. I tried to open the paper, but its creases were tight, and the paper was unusually stiff, like parchment. My fingers were just too weak.

"With your permission," the old lady said, intervening again. In a few seconds she'd taken my mug from the microwave and added both the herbal wad and a dark powder she shook from the creased paper. The mixture smelled like summer river mud to me, all eels and snail shells, but I wondered if I should trust my own senses. I took a sip. The contents tasted of pine sap and nothing more.

"Well done, young man." The old lady actually clasped her hands across her substantial bosom. "Despite your willingness to infect an entire community with disease, there is hope for you yet. You have value. Chief Washakie once told me that only foolish warriors blind their best warhorse. Many of the plains tribesmen did that, you know, ruined their horses' right eyes so they could mount them more quickly. Washakie resisted the custom. He was an eminent man, the chief, though he refused to learn how to play a decent hand of whist. You might wish to familiarize yourself with him."

"I don't have a horse," I said, puzzled.

The old lady squared her shoulders, her eyes dark and moist and peeved behind her glasses. I had clearly disappointed her with my response. "You are most welcome, sir," she said sternly. And I watched her flee the lounge in dignified haste, long skirt swishing, the large knot of her braided white hair receding like a moon.

"Hey," I yelled through a rapidly improving throat. "You forgot your book." I picked up the large mustardy-colored volume she'd left behind, noting its heft and the fact that it was written in a language I didn't recognize. By the time I made it to the doorway, the woman had vanished. I was oddly sorry to see her go.

I remember finishing the pine-sap tea. After that, events get sketchy. The next thing I really know is that I woke up in my own apartment at 4:00 p.m., and I was 98.6 degrees of appetite and energy. Cured. Thriving. Ready to hang out with friends. There was a message on my answering machine from Dr. Illium, asking me to call as soon as I could. He wanted to know how I was feeling, if I was worse or better, because my swab—which had been "festering right along" in his words—had somehow been misplaced in the lab. It had completely disappeared.

Sukie's softball game was at five. Her team won, and the players decided to celebrate at Mingle's—no men, please. That was how I ended up deconstructing pitchers of red ale at the Alibi with Marty Plover, a stocky, freckled engineer who was married to the third basewoman. I liked Marty. He had lousy taste in music, but his pungent sense of humor made him good company, especially when the talk turned to politics or sports. We spent a whole pitcher lambasting the state's new governor.

"How the West Was Bought and Sold," scoffed Marty. "This guy doesn't have a planning agenda any longer than his ranch's irrigation ditch. And he loves to subcontract good jobs out of state."

Marty was trying to establish a business in road and bridge design. He was a little bitter.

"I know what you mean," I said, even though I'd never held a real job.

"It's enough to put sweet Laralee off the idea of having a baby, she gets so mad." Marty slurped foam from the top of his pint glass. "That ticks me off. You and Sukie think about babies?"

The Post-Game Drinking Code developed by and for American males expressly forbids serious conversation, so I wondered if I'd missed something. "Sukie and I aren't married," I reminded him.

"That's not what I asked. I asked about babies. Children."

"We're still in school."

"Yeah, yeah." Marty waved a freckled hand as if he were looking for a fly to swat. "Always an excuse. Laralee said you were probably a Sagittarius. I'll bet she's on the damn money about that."

I wasn't a Sagittarius. I also wasn't sure how to handle a belligerent Marty Plover, especially since it was his turn to pay the tab. "I'm not trying to make excuses. I don't think about kids."

"Well, you ought to." The freckled hand slammed onto the table. "That's your problem. You don't think about other people and what they might be able to tell you." Marty leaned forward, his hot breath rippling the beer in my glass. "Want to hear a joke?"

I was glad for the distraction. "Sure."

"It's kind of long. I just heard it today. There's this guy, see, and everybody calls him Mosquito, and he lives with his grandma, and one day he bites his grandma and sucks out all her blood until she dies."

"This is a joke?"

"We're getting to the funny part. You'll see." Marty straightened in his seat. "So this Mosquito guy gets into this boat he has—I guess he went down to a marina or something, I didn't ask about that part—and he starts crying to everybody about how he's lost his beloved grandma. After a while, this guy called

Coyote—must be a Mexican, name like that—he asks Mosquito what's up. Coyote's in another boat, I think. Maybe they're both out fishing. Anyhow, Mosquito talks about how he took great care of his grandma, always bringing her groceries and stuff, but she got sick and died, and he misses her so much he can't stop crying. Now this Coyote, he knows better right away. He gets what really happened to Grandma. 'Why don't you have a ham sandwich?' he asks. 'Some food might make you feel better.' But Mosquito, he's got a taste for only one thing now, so he says no. 'I got some good beer back at my truck,' says Coyote. 'How about we put in to shore and cheer you up with some drinks?' But Mosquito doesn't go for that either. Coyote raises the ante again. 'A barbeque at my house then. With the wife and kids. I got a houseful of polite, juicy kids.'

"Mosquito can't resist that offer. Coyote gets in touch with his family—by cell phone, I guess, the gal who told me this didn't say—and Coyote asks his family to lay out a nice spread in the backyard. He also tells his wife that she and the kids need to make their noses bleed and fill some bowls with blood and leave the bowls on the picnic table with the food."

Marty squeezed one eye shut as if sighting me from the wrong end of a telescope. "You getting this so far?"

"Sure," I said. "I'm just waiting for the part about the rabbi and the priest."

Marty, who acted like he hadn't heard me, went on. "They have a nice meal. Hamburgers and potato salad, all that good stuff. Everybody pretends not to notice Mosquito greedily slurping their blood from the bowls whenever he gets the chance. When Mosquito is happy and bloated, Coyote yells from the front of the house, 'Hey, bud. The marina just called. Your boat's out of its slip.' Well, Mosquito hauls ass out of the house because he loves that boat, but he's wobbly from being full of blood, so he trips going out the door and falls, and he pops like a balloon."

Marty waited a beat, then showed me all his teeth. "Like a balloon," he chortled. "He pops. Splatters. Just like a dog tick."

"Yeah," I said, thinking Marty should stick to light beer. "That's . . . original. Where'd you hear it?"

"Huh?"

"Who told you the joke?"

"Oh. I got it off the Internet at work."

"But you said some gal told it to you."

"I did?" Marty scratched at his short, spiked hair. "I guess it must have been that girl at lunch. I was at Rose's. I like the fried rice there. Girl next to me at the counter told that joke. She was wearing one of those hippie granny skirts and some super-retro glasses, but she had great hair."

"You noticed her hair?"

"Yeah, I bet it goes down to her knees when it's loose. She wore it all twisted up in a bun, like Laralee does when she plays catcher."

My pulse got thready. Hair in a bun? A granny skirt? Those were bizarre coincidences. "So she was a student," I said, reassuring myself. "She was young?"

"She didn't look *that* young." Marty thought hard. "She was carrying a big, thick book. And she said she knew you—I remember that, now that you mention it. She brought up your name. Said she knew you pretty well."

I repressed the urge to gulp. The idea that someone suspiciously like the old lady from the AHA lounge had mentioned me to Marty freaked me out. It shouldn't have, but it did. I got to my feet, paid for the beer, then headed to my apartment on Custer Street, certain that my recent illness had softened my brain. I left a message for Sukie letting her know I was probably having a relapse, then crawled under the blankets on my mattress to the sounds of Counting Crows. I tried to relax. I tried to remember what the old lady had said to me that morning. Books, fever, women with their hair in buns. There couldn't be a connection, could there? And what difference did it make if there was? When I finally fell asleep, I expected to dream. I hoped to dream. Instead, I went into that weird suspended state where you feel like a carcass dangling from a spider's web. The whole night was about as comfortable as an ass-busting mountain descent on a cheap hard-tail bike.

I was at the door of the AHA as soon as it opened. Using the back stairs, I was able to infiltrate the Bedard Collection without signing in at the desk. I'd had several hours to consider the events of the previous day. The trouble, I decided, had begun with the assault of the falling book. I was going to give that book a dose of its own attitude.

But I couldn't find the damn thing. It wasn't where I'd left it. In fact, I couldn't locate a yellow book on any of the shelves. I checked study tables. I looked under heaped newspapers. I wiped cobwebs out of corners. Nothing. The book was gone.

Frustrated, and more than a little worried about my sudden passion for wild goose chases, I took a break. A meager dose of light leaked through the one fourth-floor window the adminis-tration hadn't managed to brick over in the name of "architec-tural rehabilitation." As I basked in the diluted sun, I eased my backpack from my shoulders. This caused a pair of Frisbee golf discs—the driver and my best putter—to slide onto the grimy floor. Why the hell not, I thought. I hadn't gotten anywhere obey-ing the rules.

I hefted the discs, closed my insomniac eyes, and let 'em rip. I followed the blue driver deep into the stacks, picked it up, then checked the books in the immediate vicinity. Nada. Three throws later, however, I scored one for the home team with a slicing putt.

The spine of the book wasn't really yellow anymore, don't ask me why. But it was the same heavy bastard. The marbled endpapers were a dead giveaway. The copyright page had been cut out, but the title page was intact. It read:

INDIAN SUPERSTITIONS
As Recalled By
The Devoted Pupils of Breakell Institute
United States Indian Training School
Camp Brown, Wyo.
1906

A table of contents listed sections on Creation Myths, Animal Stories, and Legends & Folk Tales, but there was no such material in the body of the book. Instead, what followed was hundreds of pages of hand-scrawled ledger entries. What little I could decipher was boring as hell:

> [*illegible*] shoes   7 Pr   4Pr brown
> linen—frm St Marys, Denver   37 sets, 11 spoild
> 225 lbs beef (dried) to Washakie & Redman & Spotted Calf

I slammed the book shut, disgusted with myself. My troubles, if I really had any, were in my fever-filleted brain. The book had nothing to do with anything. I gathered my discs and headed toward the front desk, where I could hear Lacy Proffit whistling a Bette Midler tune. When I exited the stacks, I found her on the floor doing Pilates stretches. She didn't seem surprised to see me.

"GETTING INTO THE RESEARCH, HUH?" She had to shout to hear herself above the music on her iPod. "THAT SEEMS TO HAPPEN UP HERE."

"Not to me," I demurred. "Can I ask you a question?"

"SURE. WHAT I'M HERE FOR." She punched a button, then sat upright, struggling to cover her ample midriff with a white peasant blouse. Her eyes were crooked with blue eyeliner.

"Ever seen this book before? It hasn't been cataloged."

"Hmmm." Lacy pulled a pair of daisy-trimmed reading glasses

from a holster on her hip. "No, but . . ." She thumbed through the inky pages. "This looks like her handwriting. It must be one of the Breakell Institute's bookkeeping ledgers. I've never really looked at them."

"Her?"

"You *know*," Lacy said, smiling raffishly. "Big Bad Fanny."

"Fanny?"

Lacy sighed. "Your benefactor. My boss. The One Who Overlooks Us All, or she did until last night. I found her portrait behind the coatrack this morning. It must have fallen off the wall. Take a look." She lifted a large, dingy, amateurish oil painting from behind her desk. I didn't have to read the brass identification plate. I knew the face all too well. Grace Frances Bedard, 1847–1932. She was my buddy from the downstairs lounge.

I took the longest, sweatiest bike ride I could manage. While I skated the slick rock below Cactus Canyon, I reviewed what I knew about Fanny Bedard. She was originally from Connecticut, the only child of a dry-goods merchant and his wife. Educated at a New York finishing school. Inspired by an Episcopal missionary to join battle against the lawless heathenism of the West. Unmarried. Friend and enemy of Native chiefs. Friend and enemy of U.S. government agents. Long-suffering school mistress who ended her days matching wits with the all-male faculty of my own small university. Ethnographer. Author of shrill letters to politicians. Bossy britches. I wondered who would go to the trouble of impersonating her, and why they would pull their trick on me.

This was the first question I had for Sukie when I met her in the student union for lunch.

"Are you sure you're not manifesting complex negative feelings about women?" she responded. I was so busy admiring Sukie's dimples that I missed the rattler's buzz between her words.

"No. I mean . . . yes, I'm not. Somebody is trying to nail me with a gigantic practical joke. I thought you might know who it is."

"Well, this woman came into my lab this morning, and we had a great talk about patriarchy. She wanted to preview some of my digital maps, the first person who's asked to see my work in I don't know how long. She told me a story that made me think of you."

"She did?"

"Yep. She said lots of cultures cultivate stories about unmarried girls who make mistakes and are brutally punished for them. It's all about controlling female bodies, the scary power of fertility. Like this one American Indian story where a girl gets up in the night, goes to pee outside her lodge, and gets back in bed. But this guy is out there—she called him Lynx—and he pees over the spot where the girl went, and this makes the girl pregnant. There's disgrace and blame and argument, all the regular phallus-centered bullshit. Then, after the baby is born, a council calls a meeting of all the men in the village. They figure the baby won't cry when it's in the arms of its dad. Well, the test works, and this girl is stuck with the sneaky Lynx guy, a poor, average-looking husband, through no fault of her own. She didn't *do* anything, and she gets hosed. The story made me mad."

"It did?"

Sukie shook her head in a way that made me feel poorer and more average looking than usual. "You bet. It's justification for neutralizing feminine power, a way to codify the marriage of 'arrogant' women to lazy dickheads as punishment."

"I guess it's good that times have changed," I said cheerfully.

"Have they?"

I decided to shift topics. "So this woman liked your maps?"

"Oh, yeah. I uploaded my overlays of state population, income, health care—all that stuff. Fran was really jamming on the visuals I've put together for the reservation. She loved those. She used to work up there."

"Fran?"

"Yeah. She's like a visiting scholar in library science or something, but she knows a helluva lot about the rez. I really liked her. We're having dinner together tonight."

"This Fran," I asked, gathering my courage, "does she have glasses and long hair?"

"She's not a hottie, if that's what you're asking. A strong face, though. Really fierce. But, yeah, she does have a lot of hair. Wears it clipped into a bun with these beaded Shoshone barrettes."

I let the sinking feeling in my stomach run all the way to my knees. "And you're having dinner with her?"

"Uh huh. And, no, you can't join us. I told Fran I wanted to hear more about her women's health ideas, so it's gals only. You wouldn't like her, anyway. Too . . . *steadfast* for your taste."

"Steadfast?"

"Plus, she's got some cool ideas about the female brain and abstinence."

"Abstinence?"

"Sure. I've been thinking about it for a while." Sukie reached over and pinched the skin on my thumb. "I was planning to talk to you. It seems like something we should try so I can stay centered for my exams. You don't have to worry, it wouldn't be *too* long. Only six months."

I did what any other honorable male would have done: I got down on my knees in front of Holly-Carol Nyquist. I had no idea why I was the object of an elaborate Fanny Bedard–flavored prank, but I was somehow certain Ms. Nyquist did. She'd given me that smile, after all. The one that hinted at trouble.

And, frankly, I was willing to do whatever it took to keep Sukie out of the nunnery.

Holly-Carol made me wait outside her office almost two hours.

By the time she opened her door, the AHA staff were rinsing out
their public radio mugs and slipping into their sensible shoes. The
building would soon be empty.

The priestess looked at me, and I looked at her, and you can
guess which of us blinked first. I told her I wanted twenty-four-
hour access to the Bedard.

"That is very much against our regulations," she purred.
"*Disciplined* scholars don't usually need that kind of time."

"Well, I've . . . I'm kinda on a roll here," I fibbed. "I've been getting up to speed on old Grace Frances herself, and my advisor, he
says obsession is a good thing, that it keeps the creative juices—"

"I rather thought the obsession was hers."

Her words came in a murmur, so I assumed I'd misheard them.
I was about to shift into a higher bullshit gear when Holly-Carol
raised one of her pale, imperious hands. "Listen up, young slacker.
I believe I know Fanny Bedard better than anyone. This is her desk,
you see. And some of the blankets that were given to her by bene-
factors on the reservation." The pale hand looped from one corner of her well-appointed office to another. "I was also fortunate
enough to buy some of her private possessions at auction not long
ago. They allow me to keep her *very* much alive."

I tried not to look too aghast. The hair-raising Nyquist smile
was back again, all gapped teeth and enamel. "You may have the
key to the reading room," she declared, as her pasty fingers wormed
an object up a length of chain that hung between her unimaginable
breasts. "On one condition."

I froze to the faux-parquet floor. I could imagine half a dozen
Nyquist-inspired conditions too, um, *disciplined* for me to survive.

"If she . . . if Fanny confides in you, you must tell me where the
journals are hidden. It will be your duty."

"Duty?" I choked. I'd pretty much outgrown duty along with
my Little League uniform.

"Oh, yes," hissed the Nyquist, pressing a warm, fang-shaped item into the palm of my right hand. "Your duty to me, to *our* kind."

I knew better than to turn on the lights. Because it was almost solstice, darkness didn't fall until ten. I tried to prepare a short speech for the Fanny impersonator I expected to sweep into the G. F. Bedard Memorial Reading Room at the stroke of midnight. I wasn't buying Holly-Carol Nyquist's voodoo babble. I wanted Fake Fanny to know I appreciated eccentricity as well as the next fellow, but she could quit with the costume drama. I wasn't a hard guy to approach. And what the hell did she want from me anyway?

"Perhaps I want to learn your lawn-party game."

The words came from nowhere . . . and everywhere. I was sitting on top of Lacy Proffit's extremely clean desk.

"Huh? Wha'?" I'm not the most articulate fellow when I'm spooked.

"The athletic endeavor to which you are so devoted. With the spinning platters. Perhaps I just want to learn how to play." An indistinct figure with a very distinct voice emerged from the gloaming of the stacks. It seemed to be my friend from the lounge.

"Uh, yeah. Frisbee golf. I can do that." The figure moved close to me, then closer. It appeared to advance without benefit of moving its legs.

"Miss Fanny Bedard," she said, holding out her right hand. I took it, my heart flailing between excitement and fear. The hand was as cool and substantial as it had been the day before.

"I . . . I'm honored, I think."

"You should be. There are important people who wish they were in your shoes."

"There are?"

"Yes. I don't do this very often."

"Do what? Pretend you're a ghost?"

She laughed, a slash of humor across what was indeed a fierce face. "Is that what you think? That I'm a pretender?"

"Yeah. Yes, ma'am. The real you has been dead more than seventy years. Your portrait confirms that." I pointed to her rehung likeness on the wall.

She sidled closer to me. She smelled like Sukie had the day before—of sagebrush and wood smoke. "I've always abhorred that picture." She laid a chilly hand on my shoulder, and I felt myself go giddy. The hand remained in place. The giddiness increased. When I bumped my head against the sprinkler system, I realized we were both suspended high above Lacy Proffit's desk, riding the air like a pair of two-legged clouds.

There's really nothing more to say. As a former comic-book addict, I have a strict set of standards when it comes to superpowers. Fanny met the standards.

"I believe you've known what I am from the start," she said, with some pride. "It's an endearing trait—the fixed limits of your intelligence. You haven't been a waste of effort."

"A waste?"

"Oh, rather. The last one—a mangy redhead with piercings in her nostrils—she only wanted to know if I was what's called a dyke. She was writing a paper for one of her history courses. You, on the other hand, have been an adequate pupil."

"I have?"

She nodded, the split lenses of her glasses glinting from silver to gray. "Your immune system recovered nicely."

"The fever, the sick part? You did that to me?"

She shook her head. "I don't *do* much of anything. The book made its own decision. I merely kept an eye on you. Some of the volumes in here can be quite . . . forceful. I thought giving you a case of smallpox, however appropriate, was a bit much. I lessened the effects."

I touched my forehead. The bruise there, at least, still felt very real. "And what did the book decide? What did it want? I couldn't make much sense of the damn thing. Your handwriting sucks."

That got to her. Even ghosts like to maintain certain proprieties. I felt a very sharp pinch at the back of my neck, though Fanny ostensibly kept her spirit hands to herself. "The book merely wants respect, all that any of us asks for. There are quite a few of the old stories housed among its pages—stories you are barely able to recognize because of your immature predilections. The book wants us to remember its stories. Someone, I hope, will eventually give the children of the Breakell Institute, of all Indian schools, their due. We thought that's what we were doing back in my day, teaching farming, teaching English. Everyone tried very hard." Fanny sighed. "But our education policies became manacles and chains. We left behind a miserable mess. I have finally been dead long enough to know what it feels like to lose your entire way of life, your culture, your home. It's a terrible theft."

I didn't know what to say. Fanny Bedard was expressing grief for actions that contemporary scholars had loudly condemned. The Indian school policies she'd helped implement were gone. What good did it do to feel guilty about it all?

"The good," she said, reading my mind as I might have expected, "comes as a result of the guilt. One is prodded to shift one's perspective and analyze past mistakes. You ought to try it sometime."

I recognized a familiar knot in my stomach. "Are you about to give me an assignment? Do I have to write about you or something?"

"Good heavens, no." Fanny actually snickered. "You're not nearly devoted enough for such a task. I have my eye on a young Nebraskan in the sociology department for that."

"What's my gig then? You really want to toss some Frisbees?"

"Later. I have a simple request. The Nyquist, as you so tenderly think of her, has taken something from me. I want it back."

"But she says *you* have something *she* needs. Journals or something. Did you hear us talking about all that? Were you, like, hanging around in the walls?"

Fanny made a sound like sandpaper rubbed on cement. "I heard her, the old bitch. She's still hoping to find my journals, but I burned them all on their own deserved pyre."

"Why would Nyquist care about your journals?"

"Because, unlike you, she's properly curious. And ambitious. The newspapers of the day made quite a scandal out of my maiden lifestyle among the red men. They trumped up all sorts of liaisons and fleshy conveniences. The folderol eventually undercut much of my truly useful work on the reservation. A pity."

"And it was all lies?"

"I did not say that." There was another sly pinch at my neck. "Let's just say the bonds I formed were considered honorable among my hosts."

"So what's Nyquist got on you?"

"Knickknacks. Emblems of vanity. She purchased my sterling comb-and-brush set from my grandniece's estate a month ago. She reckons they give her some power over me."

"But they don't, right? You can just do the haunting thing, really piss her off?"

Fanny Bedard removed her bifocals and glared at me. I understood how she'd once cowed an entire faculty.

"Okay. I'm wrong. I guess you need me to get the goods from the Nyquist. A simple burglary. A not-so-terrible theft?"

Fanny nodded.

"And my incentive is?"

A spacious grin filled her face. She reached for something that hung from the beaded belt around her waist. It looked like a pair of musty dried figs. "A gift for your most excellent lady friend from my mentor, the shaman Winter Willow. It is said to make the female quite amorous."

I stole the silver comb and brush from Holly-Carol Nyquist's office the next afternoon when the AHA suffered a mysteriously malfunctioning fire alarm. I left the items deep in the bowels of the Bedard Collection on top of the once-again yellow copy of *Indian Superstitions*. The boar-bristle hairbrush was still tangled with strands of very long, unfaded brown hair. I thought about filching a strand or two, but didn't. The rest of the summer, including actual research on my dissertation, advanced without incident except for two occurrences: The next time I saw Holly-Carol Nyquist she was wearing a large turquoise turban due to permanent, overnight hair loss that her allies attributed to stress. The Nyquist pretended not to recognize me. This was the same week I defended my Frisbee golf title during a sudden-death play-off against a lanky physics professor. I won thanks to a hotly disputed call made by the young referee no one had met before. She wore gold-rimmed glasses, and her hair, mostly hidden by a purple bandanna, was braided into a magnificent bun.

Oil & Gas

Primex Corporation
Badger Springs IV (under construction)
51N, 74W

Why do we always got to wait for the electric?

Because it's Headquest. And Headquest and them, what's that journeyman's name, the one always talks about being in the navy—they're busy. They run late.

We're busy. I can hear the boss taking a verbal bite out a your ass now. Time is money. *Your* time is *my* money.

Yeah, he's real original that way. Rather be here than in the shop, though. Monica can find me in the shop.

You had a decent phone plan like that Verizon, she could find you now.

Rather she didn't.

Am I asking why?

Get yourself married and you'll find out why.

You wish you'd studied electric?

Sometimes. Money's good. I took one class at the college when I thought I was going for the railroad. Uncle said he could get me on the B&N, but he couldn't. Welding's okay, I guess. I got the eyes for welding. And you work outside most of the time. Like this.

Eat a lot a dust out here.

You eat dust. I don't get all that shit in the windows when I drive.

I'd like to have my rifle right now. Sweet little .270 I got, all sighted in. I'd take that whitetail down. He's been staring at us since we got here.

That's a buck for you. On parade like a rooster till hunting season opens.

You know the Texan works with the pipe fitter, tall guy who's got about seven fingers left on his hands? He poached a doe couple weeks back. Jimmy Goehring told me about it. He got fresh steaks out a the deal.

Whatever. Change the radio, will you? I'm sick of her songs. She's got nothing to say. A man that hunts out of season ain't no kind of man unless his family's starving. That's my granddad's rule.

No Texan that works for R.M.E is starving.

Then he's a asshole.

Asshole with his freezer full, what I'm saying.

Join him if you want. But you can't use my pistol. Pistol's for snakes.

I ought a go looking for snakes. I'm bored as hell. Helping that old lady stomp out that brush fire woke me up before I was ready.

That was all right, wasn't it? Lending her a hand. She needed a little help. And it beats slopping salsa at Taco John's. God, I don't miss that.

Beats mucking trench lines like that college kid Mr. Parmalee brung in. Poor son of a bitch. Somebody hung his luck around a rabbit's neck. He gets all the shit jobs. He ain't been out of the mud yet.

I don't know. Bet he's got it all right when school's in. Probably even gets laid now and again.

The girls in Laramie ain't that hot. I know 'cause my cousin's one a them. Billings is way better for girls.

The Mint is better than that if you don't mind shelling out for a shitload of mai tais.

Colored drinks turn my stomach. Can you explain to me why girls like them colored drinks?

Vodka shooters. Monica and her best friend get real slippery on vodka shooters.

That the friend got a heart shape to her ass?

That's the friend with the husband who pays attention. I'll give you some free advice this morning, since you're listening. You don't want even one whiff of that Tracy Schuster.

I'm not on a fishing expedition or nothing. Just recording the fact she's got a nice shape to her ass. Big line a dust over there. Truck's coming.

Good. Think you can keep your mind off your dick and do some work? It might be Headquest and them. In their glory.

Naw. He's stopped. Turning back, the dumb shit. Just another fool that got hisself lost on these roads.

Well, join the club, why don't he? Found and lost. I'd like to paint me a sign says that in big letters, take it everywhere I go in these fields. Found and lost. I'd like to write that up as the damn Wyoming state motto.

Emergency Room
Campbell County Memorial Hospital
Gillette, Wyoming

You'd think the hospital would be a lousy place to work. I mean we're so busy, especially on summer weekends, what with the tourists out of the Black Hills and all the field workers in here looking to lose money and find trouble. Plus the Mexicans. I'm not against Mexicans myself. My Mormon cousin over in Kaycee married one, and she's real pretty and takes good care of the kids. But it's hard with the pregnant ones. They usually haven't seen a doctor, and they've had zero prenatal except what they manage themselves. Plus they don't speak English. Most of the younger docs here carry some Spanish. *Vamanos.* I've picked up my share. We get them through. But it's harder than it has to be. That's all I'm saying.

So the story today is that we lost a patient. Not lost like died—that's not a bulletin-board item. Lost like misplaced. Like he was here in a bed being treated for dehydration and now he's not and nobody saw him leave. I asked Petra, who was supervising the ER at the time, if she checked the silverware drawer in the nurses' lounge because that's where I'm always accidentally hiding things from myself. Petra didn't think it was funny. My remark.

Lora Van Tassell brought the man in late last night. I knew her in high school. She's with the environmental department now and was collecting water samples from one of those drainages they're drilling the hell out of. Fortification Creek, that's the name. The drainage, not the man. We don't know the man's name. He didn't have ID. No wallet, nothing. Just the clothes on his back. Dressed like a rancher, that's what the alert says. They don't have a picture. The police would've taken a picture this morning, but they got here too late. Petra thinks methamphetamine dealers robbed the old man, which was why he was so out of it. She thinks that drug is behind every single thing that goes wrong around here. Which it practically is. The pregnant ones on meth are the worst. They smell bad with bad teeth, and the babies twitch like peeled frogs. Poor things. And the STDs those girls are passing around, don't even get me started on those.

Lora Van Tassell was the only one awake enough to get a good look at the man. She told Petra he looked familiar to her, like maybe she'd seen him at her grandmother's church over in Buffalo. The Catholic one. Her grandmother's big into that. But Lora wasn't going to drive ninety miles on a Friday night to find out if the man was Catholic. Besides, something wasn't right. There wasn't blood or chest pain or any of that. The ER did an exam. He just wasn't very responsive, and when he did talk the words weren't quite in English. Spanish either, according to Lora.

Could be he's a sheepherder. We used to get them from all over, even South America. Some of them will go right out of their heads from the loneliness that comes with sheep. Some of them handle it fine. But they don't run sheep around the Powder River like they used to. It's too hard what with low meat prices and all the exploration foolery around that natural gas. Now the fences get took down. And the roads get tore up. And the water's not where it's supposed to be. Ranching is taking a hit. But the town smells of bright green money, I can tell you that. This hospital, too. Lots more have got insurance to go with their jobs. Town times are good. People are glad for the boom. The countryside doesn't smell like much more than dirt when you go out that way for a drive, though. Dirt and diesel fuel stink. I used to love driving out toward the river. Now there's whole sections on this side of the breaks that don't look any better than a ripped animal hide. I'm still getting used to that.

Cedar Draw
Echeta Road
51N, 75W

He's not that late. Surely Lora will still be there. Eight thirteen by the dashboard clock. That wrong turn cost him five, six minutes, goddamn all the new roads out here. A man can't find his way around the oil and gas fields except by helicopter anymore. Not that it was so great in the old days. Topo maps were always for shit when it came to these roads.

He wishes he could pull up with this song on the radio. He'd bet a dollar Lora likes this song.

He would've been on-site at 6:00 a.m. if she had asked. Or earlier. Even if it is a Saturday. Let Delaney bitch all he wants. Delaney's got nothing to complain about. More than fifty well permits were approved last week. Bitch, bitch, bitch. Did he really think the state environmental people were going to do his ballroom dance forever? Delaney loves to whine through his laundry list of complaints. How he should've donated more money to the Democrat who ran for governor. How he should've set up smaller partnerships, kept to his bold core of investors. How he should've locked horns with the environmentalists. Instead, he claims he's missed his chances and lost a bank full of money. The jerk. Delaney's doing fine. Delaney's not hurting. And his outfit's stayed out of court, more or less.

He can't believe Lora Van Tassell isn't married. With that figure and a brain to go with it. His body's still in pretty good shape. No belly yet, he works on that. Will she care that he's divorced? He doesn't want to soft-pedal his commitments or his mistakes, it's taken a lot to get him back in the saddle again, but Rosie was born a devoted Seventh-Day Adventist; eighteen years of marriage never got them past that. No kids. That's part of what went bad, and he's sorry for it. Sorry for Rosie. She'd make a great mom. He's been checked out by the doctors, though. He did that much for Rosie. If there's ever a need, he's still capable of making babies.

Geez, he needs to watch his thinking. Thoughts like that are low territory even if he hasn't been on a date for more than a year. Phil Triplek, one of the engineers on this project, has already gotten out of hand with the Viagra jokes.

Almost there. Looks like one truck raising dust up ahead of him. Wrong color vehicle, though. Definitely not Lora's.

It's just like her to want to walk the site again. He's got the latest grids. He thinks he can convince Delaney to plan for reinjection of the well water if that's what Lora and her bosses recommend.

The lens they want to tap is sweet water, worth saving instead of just spilling out onto the ground. And they need to get ahead of the curve on water reclamation, that's his opinion. Set some new industry standards. The roughshod days are nearly done. It's time for the coal-bed methane biz to grow up. Triplek thinks the hammer's coming down soon anyhow because of the sage grouse problem, no matter what. The grouse are disappearing from this part of the state even faster than good groundwater. Everybody, even the feds, has noticed that.

One thing he's learned in this trade is how to go lean and mean. He'll be direct with Lora. It's a chance he can't waste, him out of Casper, her operating out of Gillette. Dinner tonight? Coffee sometime soon? Hell, he'll drive seventy-five miles to buy her coffee. It'd be worth it. His blood hasn't fizzed like this in he doesn't know how long. She wears her ponytail out the back of her cap. Long, tan legs in hiking shorts. All business and smarts with a good sense of humor. She even likes football. Goddamn, he needs to rein in. Not think about Lora in those shorts. If he keeps this up, Triplek and the other engineers will have to hold him down and reinject him with common sense. Just to relieve the pressure.

Kinney Divide
Maycock Road
50N, 76W

Fuck it, Tonto. Try the wires again.

Give me a minute. I got a lot of grease here.

Goddamn truck, I hate it. I hate a goddamn Chevy.

Just settle for two minutes, Jason. I'm about to get her right.

Why isn't dickhead helping us? Where's he gone to? The wind's kicking up bad.

He's taking a leak. You want to come hold the light for me or sit up there and complain?

I want to get home. Shower. Eat a T-bone steak before my Friday night's disappeared. My hand hurts like hell.

Think you broke it? Or can you hold this light?

I'm coming. It's swolled up some, see? Aches like a son of a gun.

You might've chipped a bone in that knuckle. I did that once. Healed after I wore a splint for a few weeks. Okay, set that there while I check the connection on this wire.

You gonna report it? My hand?

I got to report it unless you want to miracle-heal yourself with ice. Insurance requires.

Quealey ain't gonna like it.

It was a accident. I saw it. You didn't fuck up or nothing, so you should be fine.

I fucking hope so. 'Cause I'm still peeing in a bottle for that fucking county judge. I've had my problems. I admit it. But I need this job. Really need it. I'll haul my share of pipe without a splint if I have to.

I'll talk to Quealey. You're doing good. Is Prentiss back yet? Prentiss, we need that flashlight you got unless you want to camp here till dawn. What's he doing out there so long? Wishing on stars? Prentiss!

I can't see him, the loafer. It gets darker than you'd think up in these hills. Cold, too. Want me to try dispatch again? Let 'em know we're down?

Good luck. I couldn't get nothing but crackles. We might as well be on the moon. Get up in the cab and put the clutch in, will you? Then wait for my say.

Okay. But I'm about ready to kill that Prentiss. Drive off and leave his ass, that's what we ought to do. That's a real storm coming in.

Maybe he scared hisself with that story.

What story? The car wreck he told about, the one with his aunt and his sister?

You don't listen good, do you? Try the ignition one more time. My hand hurts. It's a distraction.

That almost got her. Turn it again. Shit. One more wiggle on this wire maybe. Yeah. Yeah, that's it. I'm talking about the Chinese story.

What Chinese? Was he talking about being laid off again, from the mines? I'd like to get on at a mine someday. Everybody would. Best pay in the world, hail to the fucking unions.

I don't know what he said about no mines. He's from Rock Springs, right? Only been here a few months. He said he saw a Chinese today.

So? There's all kinds out here. Fortex has got guys from Russia working on their lines.

Uzbekistan's what you're thinking, the ones with Fortex. Uzbeks. It was when we left him at that gate, so he could wave in that load of pipe. He said he saw a Chinese guy swinging an old-timey lantern, the kind that burns kerosene. In the daylight.

God*damn*, I hate a piece-of-shit Chevy. You had it for a second.

Yeah. Motherfuck. Yeah, yeah—yeah! Hold her there, Jason. That's it. Good. Let it run just like that for a minute. I'm going to holler for Prentiss and his Chinese. He says a thing like that means a coal mine's about to cave in, or something bad's gonna happen. It had him thinking. It's a story they believe in Rock Springs.

We ain't in Rock Springs. We're headed home for steak. At least I am.

Prentiss is weird, in case you hadn't noticed. You might want to hit the horn to call him back in here.

I hope he's got the sense to come in before that lightning gets any closer. That batch looked rough. I don't need a Chinese man to spook me home. Rain'll do her. I can't afford to get stuck in no gumbo out here during the rain, not with a weekend of tequila medicine in front of me. No fucking way. You know how I hate gumbo roads. No Chinaman's gonna change that.

I hear you. I've about paid out all my patience, too.

Then let's tear up the road to home, Tonto. What say? There's traffic out here now and again. I vote we leave Prentiss with his thumb up his butt and tear it on home. It's barely dark. There's traffic.

I don't know. Maybe you're right. Maybe. Ain't much that can happen to the lazy son of a bitch, is there? He's got his coat and stuff. What ever happens to anybody in Wyoming? A whole lot of nothing.

Cedar Draw
Echeta Road
51N, 75W

She's late. She'll go as far as the Soft Water Creek turnoff, she should be able to look down on the site from there. If somebody's waiting, she'll go on in. But she's running way behind. Overslept. Right through her alarm. Something she never does. Then the hospital calls, wanting information on the old guy she found at Fortification Creek last night. What information? He looked like he needed help, and she helped him. Nothing special about it, though it's true she doesn't make it a regular practice to pick up men when she's working alone. But this one looked different. All pale and wobbly like he didn't recognize his own self. He seemed thankful. He was real polite to her in his way.

She hopes Delaney isn't out here tapping his toes, checking his expensive watch. Delaney loves to chap her ass. He says it every time: the role of government is national defense. Meaning regulators like her are a hindrance to American enterprise. As if she didn't come up with Delaney and his brother in school, knowing them when their family ranch went belly-up and his father crab-walked into a job at the mortuary. Jerk. Delaney likes to hear the sound of his own voice. He thinks he's become something.

If she's lucky, Andy Josling will be there to keep the peace. Andy has a reputation for being able to talk Delaney out of some of his trees. He's a good hydrologist, too. He reminds her of Dr. Lockwood from the university when he talks all steady and slow. And he's cute. She's already admitted that much.

What she wouldn't give for a state truck that played CDs. A morning like this deserves good music, not this punch-card stuff on the radio. Word is that Andy likes to dance. She can see that in the way he walks. One thing she's always liked about older guys is how well they dance.

She wishes she hadn't checked her messages while her cell phone was still in service. Danton always calls on weekends. She knows that. She should've been ready. He said he was in Oregon for the rest of the month, catching the last snow on Mount Hood. He said he was doing good, maybe she wanted to come out? The way he asked the question just about made her cry. He didn't mention Chelsey, it was probably some other girl by now. Chelsey was the kind who would split.

God, his voice. And he was sweet to the bone, so good looking and athletic. She didn't regret a single minute of those two years in Jackson. They'd had great times, a few of them wild. It wasn't the girls that killed her. She'd tried to explain that to him. It was more that she wanted to move on—if going back home was any kind of moving on. She had a great job offer, the work was interesting. Gillette was no kind of place for a competitive snowboarder, she knew that. He wasn't supposed to follow her. It was just time. Danton said he'd stop to see her on his way through to visit family on the reservation. She knows he's as good as his word. And she knows she'll ask him to spend the night. Which will be nice. She's only had sex twice since Christmas, both times with an EPA guy from Denver. It hadn't been great.

Dust from a truck coming her way? Or was that smoke? There'd been plenty of lightning last night, with wind and thunder. It was a strange night even before she picked up that old man. She hoped he was all right, wherever he was.

Danton. Lord, it was uncomfortable thinking about him. Not totally in a bad way, but still. He was doing right by himself, always making time to see his mom and aunties over in Pine Ridge. And he had a true gift for snow. They'd laughed about that some, how it was his special Lakota medicine. He was proud. But she'd never quite seen herself as part of it, his gift. Which was one reason she'd parted ways.

A green truck? Was that right? The air out here sometimes bent things into crazy shapes and distortions. You couldn't always be sure you were seeing what you saw. What she wanted to see down there to the south of that dry wash was a nice blue truck. Andy Josling's was blue.

Sawbuck Ranch
Felix Wash
51N, 74W

I'm not buying an Appaloosa ever again. If I've told Maggie May that once, I've told her a hundred times. An Appaloosa is pretty if you can get past those drowned-looking eyes, but that's all they offer. They don't stay sound. Their skin goes to rash at the slightest thing. And these ones, the three we're out here to corral, they're so dumb they practically qualify for genius. Seems like they keep me in fits most of the time.

Maggie May's got a good hand with them this morning. That mustang she's riding, I bought him at auction over in Cody. He's the horse you want. Leg bones like steel, appetite like a hungry soldier. A mustang will not go picky on you. They even beat out a mule that way. I wish I felt up to keeping him rode like I should, but my hips are no better than a spaniel's. I need to go easy, pick my spots. Maggie May's a topnotch stand-in, I'll say that. I couldn't have ordered up a better grandchild.

That little prairie fire didn't scare her a bit. We saw the smoke as far out as Lone Tree Butte, figured there was some kind of burn-off at one of the wells. But it was flames right here on my deeded section. Them Appaloosas, they didn't move with the wind like the pronghorn and mule deer will do. They decided to race about two hundred yards south so they could stand in the muddy swale. It was like they knew it was early Saturday morning and time for me and Maggie May to come to the rescue, the dumb clucks. Maggie May drove them clear with the mustang, and I got the rural fire service on the radio, just for their information. Fire burned out before it even crossed the two-track. We tamped on it with a shovel until we got just the help we needed from a welding crew that drove by. Two nice boys from up at Sheridan. It's a good thing last night's weather brung us a little rain.

Then it's Lora Van Tassell pulling up in her state truck, saying hello. I had her in sixth grade and in eighth. Smart little thing. And she never did let the attention that went to her football-star brother get under her skin. He tore up his knee at Colorado State like most of them do. Came back and tried to work for his daddy. Left for California after that. I suspect it's a good thing he didn't go through the trapdoor of marriage to that Engelheim girl he dated. I suspect marriage to any girl is not his line.

Lora's drawing pay from the environmental department, and I say good for her. The fools at the water conservation district should have been screaming at the governor for more of her kind five years ago. We could've used the help when the gas rigs started sprouting like dandelions. We could've used some common sense, too. I don't know why ranchers and farmers always think they know all there is to know, but I'm guilty of it myself. Tommy France, my husband, was better at planning for change, God rest his soul. It was an attitude he brung back with him from the Pacific and that hard fighting against the Japanese.

Lora wants to know if I've seen any trucks from Peter Delaney's outfit, DBD or whatever they call it. I haven't. There was that welding crew from Sheridan. And a blue Toyota 4x4 with Natrona County plates. Lora lights up when she hears about that one. Barely keeps her smile to herself.

She mentions a fellow she picked up last night on what we used to call Charger Road. How she took him to the hospital in town and how he slipped out again. I tell her I've never known a soul to live year-round out that way, but it's practically summertime, and it could be he's a Basque sheepman, that was their kingdom once upon a time. Those old coots have pretty much let the air out of their wagon tires by now, same as me, but maybe one of them has got to wandering. I ask Lora if she saw any swamp gas last night. Maggie May and I saw some before dawn this morning when the conditions were still right. That's another thing about my grandchild. She's not afraid to get up in the dark, and she's not tethered to the TV.

My father used to see swamp gas fairly regular when he worked the Salt Creek oil fields. Spooky stuff. He said those balls of light would roll toward you across the ground like the Lord's own chariot, or the devil's, depending on who you deserved. He said the lights would draw you into making mistakes, like driving off the road or thinking there were people out there waving lamps when there wasn't nobody at all. That used to scare even some of the old-timers. Maggie May wasn't scared this morning, and neither was I. We just watched that yellowy fox fire dip and blink. We figured we were lucky to see it. I tell Maggie May it's important to maintain the eyes and habits you need to see unusual things.

I ask Lora to give her mother a hug from me. I don't see Betty like I used to since Tommy France died and I lost some of my taste for the church. Betty's the kind I miss. There's nothing judgmental about her. She's the good brand of Christian who draws in the lost lambs.

Maggie May will trailer those Appaloosas faster than I can remember their registered names. Then we'll go back to my place in town and do some practicing for the 4-H gymkhana. It's week after next. If I play my cards halfway right, somebody in the 4-H will like the look of an Appaloosa, and I can get rid of these fool hay engines once and for all.

Red Dawg Bar
Route 16
Clearmont, Wyoming

No lie. Andy didn't report in all afternoon. I am not shitting you. The man went right off the clock, took that Van Tassell gal to lunch at that little place, Debbie's, and lunch never ended. Betterton says he saw them when he stopped next door for gas. The place was empty except for a jukebox and the two lovebirds.

I'll be damned. Randy Andy. I'm just about jealous. Always thought of him as pretty quiet.

Maybe quiet's what she likes, though you could've fooled me. She used to go with one of the Curry boys in high school. Good-looking woman, I'll say that. Wish everybody who worked for the government was so easy on the eyes.

What? You don't get a rush staring at Mike Downs and his big gut?

I don't. How about you? His interim reports give you wet dreams?

Not hardly, Triplek. I got a perfectly nice wife, same as you.

Isn't that the truth. Andy's had a hard couple of years. This'll be good for him, even if it don't last.

Think she's a ball breaker?

Maybe not. She seems nice. She lived in Jackson for a while, shacked up with a pro skier or something like that. But it hasn't ruined her, far as I can tell.

I love how you're suddenly the expert, Triplek. You going to be this analytical when your girls start going on dates?

No way. I been on my share of high school dates. I'm locking Jen and Maddy in the attic until they're twenty-five.

Here it comes. The bullshit. You start telling lies like that, you got to buy me another cold beer.

All right. You're worth the two dollars. Then I need to head on back.

Heard anything about the kid that went missing last night?

What kid?

Wandered off from his crew when their rig broke down after dark, so his boys get pissed and lathered after a while and drive on home. Leave him out there. Bad weather, too. The sheriff reckons he spent the night curled up under a cut bank, that he'll turn up like they usually do.

He'll be fine, assuming he's not an idiot.

Those boys he works with must be idiots, so the benchmark's not too high.

There's the price of boom times for you. Nobody left to hire but druggies and thieves. Vasquez is always crying about that. He can't get good workers anymore. The Casper labor market is plumb tapped out.

It's just like the gas rush to have some kind of price tag, isn't it? I'm not a bit surprised. Wild, Wonderful Wyoming—the last place in America to get ahead, except the getting don't last.

Are you going pessimist on me again? It's not so bad. There are a few more paychecks left for us to cash.

Yeah, yeah. I just like to worry. The big-company money's moving on to Rawlins and Sublette. More power to them. They've gnawed their way through pretty much everything in this part of the state. But the speculating I see now—like what Delaney's been trying to pull—that stuff's tricky. The whole house of cards could collapse at any second.

Don't let it take you with it. That's what I say.

I won't. Sharon's real good that way. She's made us stay conservative with our money. But my kids, especially Joey, he wants to come back up here after he finishes his degree at the university. What's he going to find?

Hell if I know. Maybe he'll find what that kid who wandered away from his crew found—wind and a whole lot of nothing.

And I thought I was the pessimist.

I'm just saying there's not much you can guarantee anybody in the Land of Extraction. It's ever been that way. This state ain't got big teats to suck. You and me dug our heels in a million years ago, stuck it out like fence posts, and somehow we're still standing. We stayed stuck. Now we got a chance to ride some serious dumb luck for a while. You might want to drink to that.

Sure. Okay. Here's a cold one finished off in honor of fat field engineers. Powder River, let 'er buck.

And how about a toast to Andy Josling? He's at Debbie's Restaurant charming a pretty woman over a five-hour lunch. I can't wait to pry the details right off his lips. You and me sit here, and we talk, talk, talk about the energy business and how we're going to keep from getting screwed again, and that old boy, he's out there starting *over*. He's stopped looking over his shoulder for once. He's not sipping sad whiskey about his past. Goddamn, you got to admire the sheer balls that takes. I wish to hell I could do it. I'd pay a lot to be able to see a good road into the future. Just promise me you'll let me know if you get a glimpse of such a thing. I'd like to *see* it with my own eyes, make sure it's not another heartaching, backbreaking mirage. A real future. Goddamn.

The Little Saint
of Hoodoo Mountain

The raven shadowed her, even in her dreams.

She was sure it was the same bird each time—this is what she believed. She could see the hard, blue sky through gaps in its left wing where it had lost some of its feathers. And though it was smaller than the other ravens that lived among the spruce trees along the river, it had the loudest voice. Rusted iron against wood, that's what the bird sounded like to her. Fence post and hinge.

The raven was with her when she found the grave at the Addicoat homestead. It tapped at the beetled branches of a pine while she dug into the ruins of Joe Addicoat's cabin with frenzy and a sharpened stick. But the raven didn't watch her empty the grave. It flew north instead, alone, across the cracked kneecap of Windy Peak, where her father had recently spotted a grizzly sow foraging with her cub.

She used her rifle, a Mossberg .22, to make a sling so she could carry what she unburied at Joe Addicoat's. She wasn't sure why she took the bones. To keep them for herself, maybe. To lift them from their sad, abandoned darkness. It would just be a secret, she thought. A secret of her own, however tiny and rare.

Livia found her father at the western edge of their ranch, the Red Mask. He was talking to Hobo, a friend who managed cattle in the valley for a Salt Lake millionaire. Her father had driven the four-wheeler out to check fence, but she knew he was really keeping an eye on the campground that was less than a mile upriver. The number of campers increased every day. Forest Service employees, state archaeologists, a historian from the college, even a writer from the newspaper in Jackson. Everyone wanted a look at the bones a tourist had discovered in one of the Indian caves. The activists from WilderLands—young, rice eating, and dirty—were there, too. They'd been around all summer.

Hobo waved to her as she crossed the flooded hay field with her dog, Nock. He was a tall man with a bit of belly and a good hand with horses. He took his straw hat off his bald head, put it back on, then waved again. Her father turned. He looked thinner than ever, and tired, but he still had a strong smile for her. He hadn't forgotten that.

"Where's your fat-ass pony?" Hobo was known for his joking. Most people in the valley believed his jokes kept him employed.

"Where he's supposed to be," she said. "I been feeding bulls and steers like I was asked. Tino don't like the bulls."

Her father gave her a peck on the cheek. "How are you, Liv? Did you get breakfast? Is your ma awake?" He'd been like this as long as she could remember, careful, good mannered. What it brought him, as far as she could tell, was a clean, white dignity he could sail above his griefs.

"She got up at two, which you probably heard. Been up ever since. I left her in the garden."

"Is Playa with her?"

"Yes, sir. I made sure of that." Playa was her father's cow dog. They both believed Playa could guard Connie Eaton from things they could not.

"What's the gun for?" Hobo rebuttoned his frayed shirt-sleeves as he eyed her small rifle. Livia could see his forearms were scratched like he'd tussled with a cat or a patch of wild roses.

"That coyote lives up Fishhawk Draw. The one you're too lazy to shoot."

Hobo laughed. He had good teeth for a cowboy, though she didn't always care for the false smells of his breath. Mint gum and whiskey. "You can have the coyote, missy. I got bigger things to hunt."

Her father gave off a frustrated whistle. "We've already got one mess around here, Hobo. I hope you don't plan to make things worse. People around here, much as I love them, have a tendency to make things worse."

"I didn't say a word about shooting those damn wolves." Hobo bent to pull himself a grass stem and gave her a sly wink. "I know how to keep my business to myself."

"Uh huh. How many calves you lose last week?" Her father, she saw, was trying to maintain his equilibrium. He was better at that than anyone she knew.

"I'm happy to say not a one."

"I lost two on Gravelbar Creek that I can prove. I'm giving Tad Robinson at Fish and Wildlife another call, ask for some relief."

"Good luck to you," Hobo said, chewing on his grass. "Those wolves were in Peer Gulch in April, now they're on Hoodoo Mountain. Got more pups than I've got saddles. They'll eat their fill of your beef, then disperse clear to Nebraska before Tad Robinson lifts a hand. He never wanted them to stay in Yellowstone."

"Maybe not. But he doesn't like it when they kill calves. I can get reimbursed."

Hobo made a tolerant sound with his lips. "Money's something. I don't dispute that. But your problem might be bigger. Mick Smith over at the Double Z says the Indians are sending somebody down from Montana to pray over that cave because of what that New York fellow found in there, those bones. They're holy, I guess, like every other damn thing around here. If the Indians get in with their praying and legal claims, that'll be all she wrote. Campground'll be a circus."

"I can't worry about the campground. My lease is good. I got two hundred pair grazing over there, and I can't rotate them to Hoodoo because of the wolves. My cows are gonna stay on that grass no matter how many people think they need to hike to that cave."

"You're practicing your speech on the wrong crowd, Paul. I know your troubles. We all got 'em. I'm just saying the public land you rent around those caves is about to go *real* public."

"You love good news, don't you, Hobo?" Her father sucked on one end of his gray mustache, a thing she hated.

The other man pulled at his braided brown belt, then shrugged. "You know I'll help if I can."

Her father grunted, turned away from them both to crank up the four-wheeler. His irrigation boots had become clownish with mud. "Gotta get on it," he said, shouting over the rough hammer of the engine. "Livvy, check on your ma." And he was gone.

They both waited a long minute before they said anything. It was easier to watch Paul Eaton shrink like a thrown rock.

Hobo drew a pack of Viceroys from his shirt pocket and offered her one like always. "That boy who moved into Pextons' cabin is a guitar maker, not a artist like we thought."

She took the cigarette. "If he's storing wood, it'll get too dry on him. That's what ma says. He won't stay long."

Hobo snorted air through his hawkish nose while he gave her a light. "You don't never disappoint me, Livvy. You always act like nothing sticks around here but prickle grass."

"He'll get tired of it. And his wood won't work right." She was careful to inhale the smallest stream of smoke. She was only fourteen. Cigarettes were still new to her.

"Someday a person's gonna outlast you, missy. Gonna outlast your expectations."

"I doubt it."

"Looking forward to high school?"

"No."

"Think your dad will make a deal with WeirdoLands, or whatever they call themselves?"

"I don't know. Why you asking me?"

"They been up and down this valley, offering cash to folks who will take their cows off government land. It's a lot of money for a small rancher, and not the end of the world, neither. A man could bank the money, sell most of his herd, take a nice break. Folks around here would understand if your dad worked out a deal, the pressure he's under and all that."

"Don't lie to me, Hobo. They won't understand. They just expect it because . . ." She harnessed her words tight. ". . . because they think he's weak."

"You shouldn't say that about your dad, Liv."

"It's true. It's what they say on both sides of the river. Paul Eaton's not a real rancher, never has been. He's got a crazy wife to take care of."

"How is your mother?"

"The same. Too fast and happy to know what's going on."

"You tell her I said hello."

She nodded in what she hoped was a lazy way. Hobo folded his cigarette toward his palm, so he could flick off the burning ash. She did the same.

"You planning to visit the caves, maybe roust some of those outside troublemakers?" Hobo tried his wink on her again.

"No." She hadn't told anyone she'd caused the whole fuss. She'd hidden the child's bones in her favorite place, or she thought she'd hidden them. Then all hell had broken loose. Blame burned inside her like a furnace. "Dad wants . . . we need another calf count. I'll ride out and do that."

"You might want to leave that good dog behind when you go," Hobo said, pointing at Nock, who was soaking his white belly in a ditch. "You don't want him messing around near them wolves, even in daylight. They'll take a dog out."

"The wolves should be a long way from Cave Pasture. Nock'll be all right. He's smart."

Hobo gave a dry laugh. "We're all smart, missy. It ain't enough to save us or do us good."

"Damn it, Hobo," she said, holding the curse in her mouth because she liked its edges. "You talk like my ma."

"Well, Connie's all right in my book." He smiled, showing his teeth to the sky. Then he hitched at his mud-hemmed jeans and leaned in the direction of the new Dodge truck he was allowed to drive. "I'll shoe that fat pony of yours whenever you want me to."

"Okay. Long as you give me a lesson how."

"You're on, missy. We'll do it like a team."

She watched him spin off in a plume of dust and gravel. Hobo Larkin was lousy, everybody said so. He was sloppy, a drinker with bad timing. He was better at stories than bookkeeping or putting up hay. But he was straight with her. That was why she liked him. Last week he told her he'd been stalking some of the wolves that had migrated into the valley. Waiting for his chance. Hobo hadn't stinted on the facts with her, even though his plan could get him in big trouble. She preferred adults who lived hard with their facts.

Her mother said dreams were to be saved, written down as soon as you could get from your pillow to a pencil. But Livia almost never remembered her sleep dreams. If she could have designed a dream like she sometimes designed beaded hatbands, the dream would be about flying—soaring over the Red Mask Ranch, gliding up the silver vein of the river into the black shadow heart of the Absaroka Mountains where nobody went except sheep hunters and loners who believed it was important to walk all the way into Yellowstone Park. If she could fly like that, she'd know where the raspberries first came ripe in August. Where cow elk bedded down for the morning. Where the cutthroat trout were fat, unhidden, unhurried. She'd know the things she needed to know—the upcoming weather, what was headed into her valley good or bad—and that would be the dream, to be on the wing against surprise.

Her mother was sitting in the sun and grass on the south side of the house, near the raised beds of her garden. The beds had been meticulously weeded and raked, probably a few times. Livia smelled lavender in the air, and early mint. She saw the dog Playa lying on her side in the warm dirt of the potato hills, honey gold eyes flecked with suspicion. Her mother seemed to be making prayer flags again. Her lap was a heap of colored rags and string.

"Hello, Sis." Her mother was appropriately dressed for once, with a clean face and hair. Still beautiful. "How's your day?"

"It's all right. I fed the bulls and saw Dad checking fence. He don't know when he'll be back. Want me to start on lunch?"

"It's done. Or it will be." Her mother patted the trampled grass next to her. "Come sit a minute."

Livia felt the sharp, cold feeling that was always swinging in her chest swing again. "I got Tino and the horses to look after."

"Oh. Of course," her mother said. "That's very responsible of you. Want some help?"

"No, thanks." Livia knew how the game had to go between them. Her mother didn't really want to fool with the horses, or leave the garden, but she wanted to *be there* for Livia. That's how she said it, whether she was up or down. *As a mother, I want to be there.*

"I saw the moth again. You know, the *Hemaris thysbe*. He's very big. He sounds like a hummingbird when he feeds on the morning glories. May I call you if he comes back?"

"Sure." Livia ran through the rules in her head. How long could she leave her mother and stay at the corrals with Tino? Where should she put her gun? "I guess that'd be okay."

"I think so. I think so." Her mother was working with the fabrics in her lap again, sorting them by some system only she could understand.

"Hobo had news." Livia wasn't sure what prompted her to mention what she'd heard. She usually left it to her father to dole out information and decisions. He had the instinct for it.

"Mmmmm. What's Hobo Larkin have to say?"

"He says there's Indians want to come down from Montana and take over those bones they found."

Connie Eaton looked up at her daughter, her brown eyes rinsed clean of distraction. It worked that way sometimes—you could use stories about birds or plants or history to get Connie Eaton out of herself. She knew a lot about those things. They were what she said she believed in. "Did he say who was coming?"

"He didn't. With Hobo, it's always talk. But he's got Dad worried about what'll happen if there's people on the pasture all the time with the cows. Me, too."

Her mother brushed a few gray-blond strands of hair out of her eyes. She was wearing most of her rings—the turquoise, the jade, the coral. Livia liked it when she wore those rings. "You should be worried, Sis. It's important to feel that way."

"I don't know why everybody's got to come out here all of a sudden, making trouble. Making it harder on us. It's already hard enough." The rope of feeling swung in her chest again, cold, jerking. It made her not want to look at her mother.

"You know why people come here, Livvy. They like how the mountains look. They like the wild creatures they see, the fantasy that we can change our lives." Her mother gave one of her clucking-hen laughs. "It's what you're supposed to *do* about it that bothers you. You're just like Paul that way."

"Are you going to tell Dad what to do?" The Red Mask Ranch belonged to Connie Eaton. It had come to her through a childless aunt and uncle. On her good days, she had a lot to say about managing cattle and leases.

"If he asks." Her mother signaled something to herself with a smile. "Or when." She seemed to have found a needle amid the flutter on her lap, and she seemed to be sewing, her dirt-creased fingers jabbing and fluent. "I could make some phone calls about the bones. I have friends who might be able to tell me what's going on."

"Calls?" Livia wiped a salty hand across her mouth. Her mother was like a windstorm when she took up a cause. And her friends—she had a way of choosing poorly there, too. Livia's father had talked to her about that when her mother went into the hospital the last time, explaining how Connie couldn't be held accountable for hurting those who loved her most. There had been bad friends who wanted to visit the hospital. Some of them were men.

"I'll be careful, Liv. It's only the phone." The notes of the voice were light footed and sure. "I'm not so awful right now. Summer's good for me. Summer is . . . I feel as big and brave as the whole Sun Basin in summer. I promise to be careful. You can help me stay that way."

The best stories came from her mother, who had memorized them from old library pamphlets that had been typed up for dying miners and sawyers who wanted to have their say. There was the one about tricky Chief Joseph and his Nez Percé and how they snuck away from the U.S. cavalry by propping a dead warrior against the skyline to make the soldiers think the tribe was resting in camp. There was the one about the German who lost his wife to fever in the depth of winter then fed her to his pigs so she wouldn't go to waste. There was the one about the decapitated prospectors of Silent Creek who would spook your elk during hunting season if they weren't placated with offerings of rye whiskey.

But Livia didn't know any stories about Joe Addicoat. He was supposed to be a failed miner who came late to a homestead in the valley. He lived at the foot of Hoodoo Mountain all alone and was famous for his meat cache where he stored bear and elk and deer in a spring-fed pit. He lasted less than fifteen years, leaving behind a sod-roof cabin and the name Icebox Draw. One spring he was simply gone. His disappearance was not a story.

The cabin fell to rodents and the wind. Livia had hiked up there—farther than she was supposed to go on her own—to look for the denning wolves. She wanted to see where they lived, how they'd dug in and made themselves a threat to her family. But she couldn't find the den. She found the cabin instead, and the cabin interested her, then tearing up the cabin interested her because there was no one to see how angry she was. How furious. She only found the baby's grave because she was being wild. Destructive. Prying up old hearthstones for no reason. She could have left what she found behind, but she hadn't. That still bothered her. She hadn't been able to leave the child behind.

Livia opened the gate to Cave Pasture without dismounting. At least the gate was closed: hikers and hunters sometimes didn't hook the chain. She could see that most of the cows were gathered near the stock pond. Others were scattered up the narrow grassland that ran between Sheephorn Ridge and the steep yellow bluffs that were wormholed with limestone caves. She and her parents had camped at the largest cave many times. The views were good from there, and they liked spending the night where prehistoric families had rested on their way to hunting grounds along the Yellowstone

River. She'd found two unbroken spear points on that hillside, below the caves. She kept them on a shelf in her bedroom.

She could see people from the campground climbing the steep path toward the smaller cave where she'd hidden the Addicoat baby. She watched them with a stony, scorching weight in her stomach. You couldn't see that cave until you were past it, and even then, you had to use handholds in the rock to pull yourself inside. It was too small for camping, and there was no ventilation for a fire—she'd tried that. But the cave had dry chambers you could crawl into if you were slim enough, places the packrats hadn't filled with their stinky midden. She'd been stashing things in that cave for years.

The climbers were dressed in bright flag colors. They were making themselves hot and sweaty over what they thought was important.

She whistled for Nock, who trotted out of a thicket of deadfall to her left. He was a good dog, but young and apt to wander. His black-and-white chest was wet, proving he'd already been as far as Sourdough Spring. She grinned at his muddy, lopsided ears, then raised her arm and whistled again to cast him up a shallow box canyon where the more reclusive cows sometimes hid. He barked once before he raced uphill to gather the cows. Nock loved to work. And she loved to work with him.

She tallied 150 pairs of cows and calves before she was interrupted by hikers descending Sheephorn Ridge. She saw them long before they saw her, and she kept to her business, reining in and out of the woods as she checked for breaks in the fence line. But the hikers wanted to talk, one boy, one girl, older than she but still ignorant about what they were doing.

"Are you looking for something?" the girl asked. "We saw a dog running loose, on his own."

"He's with me," she said. "We're counting cows. Making sure the gates are shut." She stopped Tino but made no move to dismount.

The girl, she saw, wore a pink and blue hat with ear flaps and tassels. The kind of thing used for skiing. The boy, who had some beard on his chin, wore the kind used for baseball.

"You live out here?" the boy asked. "That's cool."

She nodded.

"It's so pretty. So unspoiled," the girl said, looking over her shoulder toward the pearled cornices of Sheephorn. "We've only been here a week and we already don't want to leave. It's way better than Yellowstone."

"Yeah," the boy said. "Camping's awesome. Especially when you get off on your own."

"You might want to be careful if you're building fires. It's been a dry summer." Livia couldn't help herself.

The boy grinned. "No fires. Rory told us about that. He's real clear with his advice. He's got us hanging our food, even our toothbrushes, high up in the trees. For the bears."

"It's a good idea. There's a sow and cub as close as Windy Peak. We've seen her."

"Rory says bears aren't a serious problem. If we're careful." The girl this time, fooling with the straps of her purplish day pack. "He talks more about boiling our water. Do you have to do that, boil all your water?"

"No," Livia said. "The ranch has good wells."

The boy asked, "Have you lived here long?"

"All my life. My ma's from the Red Mask." This wasn't entirely true, but since it should be, she said it anyway.

Both campers gave off moony, well-tended smiles. Livia could see they liked looking at her, a girl on a quick, snorty pony with a real gun scabbard. The boy, especially, kept looking at her gun. "You might know Rory, Rory Van Eglen. Tall guy. He's from Bozeman but hangs out here a lot. He found that sacred bundle."

"No, he didn't." The girl stopped chewing on the spout of a

water bottle and interrupted. "He didn't find it. Somebody else did. He's just coordinating everything. He knows Long Horse, the Indian guy who's coming, from his work in Montana."

"Whatever," the boy shrugged. Livia thought he looked like he was tired of trying to impress the girl. "She still might know him."

"I don't," Livia said. What she knew was the guy, this Rory, was in with WilderLands. One of the leaders.

"Some of us got to see it, you know. Before the archaeologists cracked down. It's really weird and powerful, like something from an ancient tomb. Most people like Rory think the paint marks on the deer hide mean something spiritual, although he knows Long Horse will want everything left alone. That's how Indians are with their stuff now. You can't blame them."

Livia heeled Tino in the ribs to square him up. He was restless, wanting to move along. "How do they know it's Indian?"

The girl was puzzled. "Well, how it looks. And where it was. They say the Arapaho tribe has stories about little people who live in the mountains like, I don't know, leprechauns? The bones are from a little person. It probably fits in with that."

"This is Crow territory," Livia said. "There's a big difference. My ma knows all that stuff. She studied it, and talked to elders. Crow in these caves for as long as anybody can remember. And French trappers."

The boy headed down the trail a few paces, not listening. Like Tino, he was bored. The girl, Livia could see, wanted to take her on but didn't quite know how to do it on her own. "I'm just saying what they say at the campground. You asked. It's a big deal—there's a meeting about it tonight. A big event for around here."

"Maybe." Livia guided Tino in a half circle, a move that edged the girl off the trail. She reminded herself it was best to be patient with people who were new to the valley. "We'll see what happens," she said. "You have a good day."

"Ever use that thing?" The boy was back. His hat was off, and she could see his hair now, how it was tangled into thick shapes that pointed at her like fingers. He was close, practically touching her rifle.

"Yep." She sealed her lips so she wouldn't sound too eager. "On coyotes. And whatever else."

"Oh. Co-yo-tes," the girl said, stretching the word into three syllables. "I . . . well, I think that's sad. That you have to shoot them."

"It's not very sad." Livia knew she shouldn't waste her exasperation on outsiders. But she was tired of these greenie kids having their ideas so easy. "Coyotes and wolves, all the predators, they take everything they can get. More than they eat. They don't go by rules."

"And that's bad?" The look in the boy's squinty eyes showed he smelled her agitation like it was a kind of spilled blood.

"Yeah, it's bad. We need to protect what we got. What my family's built up. We work too hard to feed killers for free." She said the words just the way Hobo would.

"You don't have to get mad," the girl said.

"Sure she does," the boy said. "She was probably born mad. Remember what Rory said about the marginal agriculture up here?"

The girl didn't answer. She lifted a pair of sunglasses from a strap around her neck and covered her eyes. Livia could feel the girl lasering her from behind the orange lenses of the glasses. Staring at her like she was a freak.

"I need to move on," Livia said. "I can't spend all summer vacationing like some people."

The boy snickered as Livia nudged Tino up the trail. She told herself it was a stupid encounter, nothing to think twice about. She'd held her ground. The girl was saying something now, and the words might have been a question, or even an apology, but Livia squeezed her pony into a jog as grasshoppers from the meadow leaped in buzzing arcs before her. She wasn't going to listen. Not anymore. No one she knew had ever settled anything with words.

What it looked like: boomerang shaped and wrapped in rawhide. At first, she thought it might be an army pistol. She'd heard of pioneers who buried pistols smeared with bear grease. Or gold, maybe it was somebody's stash of nuggets. Whatever it was, it had been worth something to Joe Addicoat, and it hadn't gone with him. Then she knew. She felt the pitiful truth seep through the cold dirt under her knees. It was burial, not treasure. Still, she scrabbled at it like a dog at a badger den until she could see pieces of birdy, peeled-looking bone. A baby. Some kind of mummy child. Where had it come from? How had it died? Why had it been left under the hearth? She didn't know, couldn't know. But she stole it just the same. She told herself she had a right to collect any scraps, any history, she could find.

When Livia got back from Cave Pasture, her mother wasn't in the house. She checked the garden. She looked in the family room where her mother kept a desk, but all she found was a soup pot filled with water and unlit floating candles. The best guess was that Connie had taken Playa for a walk along the river. There *was* a note from her father. He'd been called up to Cooke City to install propane tanks at one of the new summer mansions. It was part-time work that helped pay the bills. He wouldn't be back until late.

The light was blinking on their answering machine, but there was no message. They got that a lot. Her mother was the only one who pretended to be cheerful about the frequent hang-ups. She'd lean against the kitchen wall and listen to the machine's dry, abandoned hiss as if it were melody.

Livia started dinner. She fried a sliced apple in butter, then fried two brook trout. She ate what she wanted right out of the skillet because it fit her mood. The windows were open to the damp breath of evening, and she could hear doves calling to one another as they moved toward their roosts for the night. Ravens, too. The ravens were scolding something on the far side of the corrals. She hoped it was Playa and her mother. If the walk had gone well, it might not take much to get Connie settled for the night. Maybe a book of photographs and some music. Or maybe she'd want to work at her loom. Livia kicked the wooden frame with the half-finished rug trapped in its web of threads. The loom took up most of the eating space in their kitchen, and it still didn't do much good.

She called Nock to the porch and fed him his kibble and let him lick the skillet clean with his pink tongue. He pressed against her, panting, as they sat on the steps waiting for her mother.

Playa got there first. Her coppery coat was slick with mud. Connie had dirty boots and fresh scratches on her wrists. She carried a green mesh bag filled with rose hips and asters, but her chin was thrust upward as though she'd lost something just above the horizon.

"I know," she said. "I know. I know. I'm late." Her words fell like dropped pebbles from her mouth. "I'm sorry if Paul had to go looking for me."

"He went to town. It's just me." Livia, relieved, allowed herself to sound sullen.

"That's good. Or maybe it isn't. I don't know. What should I say, Liv? Tell me what to say." Connie quivered across the mouth and shoulders. She stopped talking just long enough for Livia to scale the cascade of worry that plunged straight through her belly. She had to get ready. These were the signs. Her mother was about to take a dive.

"Oh, Liv, you should have been there. We went up Skyline Trail, the one you like, just for flowers for us to have on the table, and I looked and saw the eagle, the bald eagle that fishes at the bridge, and that made me want to walk to Windy Peak, because I could put my flags up there, we all could, take a hike and a good picnic and put them, but I didn't have the flags because the calligraphy's all wrong, ruined, I ruined it, you know, I do that every time, ruin things, I can't be *patient,* and there was smoke, I saw smoke up there, clouds tearing into the sky like the clouds you spotted at Empty Lake last year, I smelled the clouds, saw them for miles, miles, miles, beautiful clouds, all that cloud space, burning across that space, all that air burning, so beautiful, why do you think it always has to burn?" Her mother's eyes blistered with tears. But she didn't cover them. Which was just like her.

Livia reached out to steady her mother like she'd seen her father do, then she moved her arms around Connie's hot, beating ribs, her own way of holding on. She felt Playa's dense, anxious weight against their legs. "It's okay, Ma. You didn't do anything bad. You got back here. It's okay." She spoke with a raw certainty she didn't trust.

It took a long, heaving minute for Connie to pull herself together. They stepped into the lit pocket of the house, and Livia poured a tall glass of water. She made her mother take the right medicine. She picked spinach from the garden because it was all Connie would agree to eat.

"I'm not sad, Livvy. That's not who this is." Connie's voice was swollen, but close to calm. "This is . . . overwhelmed, that's how I want to say it, so let's please not tell your dad."

"Ma—"

"No. This is not a warning episode. This is about feeling too much. In a good way. I know the difference."

Livia stopped stacking dishes in the sink. "There's things I'm supposed to tell."

"No. No. No. I'm asking you. Let *me* tell first."

"Like what? What do you want to tell, Ma?"

"Like the fire I saw up there. I need to call Frieda at the station and let her know."

"Oh, Ma. You shouldn't." The forest rangers were dead tired of Connie Eaton and her wildfire predictions.

"I should, because it's right. There are times when we have to tell what we know is *right*." She brought the soup pot of candles into the kitchen and began lighting the wicks. "I talked to Mark Baylor at the college. He thinks the bones at the cave are probably a hoax."

"He does?" Livia remembered Dr. Baylor as a fast talker with an earring. A man who looked at her mother with kindergarten delight.

"He didn't go into details. Wanted to meet me for lunch—which, before you say anything, I turned down. He says there are . . . inconsistencies. The artifacts haven't been in the cave very long. They were moved. That's getting the tourist who found them into trouble."

"I hope so."

"Do you really, Sis?" The question was meant to sound watered down. "You know those caves pretty well. You know what should and shouldn't be up there. Is that the kind of trouble you're after?"

"Yes." Livia held her mother's gaze. "I hope they find trouble, all of them. I want them to go away."

"Me, too? Do you want me to go away again?"

Livia took the question like a punch. "I didn't say that, Ma. I wouldn't say that."

Connie looked at her scratched wrists as if she didn't quite recognize them. "I know you wouldn't. You're not naturally mean, like some of us. So here's the *conversation* we're supposed to have. I can't tell you how to act, not anymore. There's happy in the world, and there's honest, and I want both things to be the same, but they're not. They are *not*. I suffer that truth every day. Mark—Dr. Baylor—says he thinks everyone will go home if they can establish where the bones actually came from. So . . . I wish you could see into your heart to make things easier on other people like you make them easier on me."

"I don't feel like it," Livia said quickly, her tongue fat with spit.

Her mother selected a left-sided smile. "At least you feel something. I credit Paul with that, grounding you that way. You two know exactly what to feel. It's too bad he wasn't here."

"Who? Dad? He'll be back by—"

"The moth, Livia. Are you listening to me at all? I'm telling you what's important." There were movements along her mother's jaw that Livia wasn't sure she had seen before. "I stayed by the morning glories until one o'clock this afternoon. I stayed. I waited. He wasn't there."

"He'll come back, Ma," Livia said, lullabying her words. "It's just one day. He'll be back."

"Oh, I don't think so. That part of our lives is over." Livia tried not to hear the pitch of naked pleading in her mother's voice. Connie's eyes were as hot and floating as her candles. Livia's heart twisted, then drummed. It felt like something undefended was finally drifting away from her mother on a current neither of them could see. Why did it have to happen this way, when she didn't know what the hell to do? Why did her father have to be gone so much? Why did her mother have to make so many escapes? She put out a hand, hoping her mother would grab on. The fingers that finally found hers were as cold as stones.

That part of our lives is over.

The biggest mountains in the range, Copper and Hoodoo and Sharp, took twilight into their teeth, and Connie fell into a clenched sleep on the couch while Livia kept hearing her mother's words. *Nothing worthwhile is ever easy.* Connie had said that, too.

She'd slotted her elbows close to her body and spoken as if she were reading from an invisible page of sentences that Livia was supposed to have memorized. Then she stopped talking. But it was clear to Livia that her mother expected something from her. She expected truth. And action.

The keys to the flatbed truck were in the barn. Livia spread a soft blanket over her mother's rigid spine, then sent both Playa and Nock into the yard, where she ordered them to stay. Nock didn't like the command, he wanted to be with her, but he'd be an extra responsibility at the campground. She had all the responsibility she could handle.

She eased the three-quarter-ton GMC down the drive, no headlights. She didn't want to announce her capitulation until she had to. She stepped on the clutch as a jackrabbit bolted across the moonbled gravel in front of her. She could hear the river over the pause of the engine, the constant wrestling of water in its bed. The river, she thought, never quit and never went manic and never pretended to be capable or wise. The river just ran its course.

When she swung onto the county road, the kenneled shape of another truck loomed clear of the shadows. It was Hobo's truck, badly parked in the willows. She hadn't heard any wolves when she left the house. Or coyotes. But that didn't mean it wasn't smart for Hobo to be out looking. She hoped he was careful.

There was still a crowd at the campground. The parking spaces were filled with unhitched trailers, SUVs, and tiny foreign cars held together by roof racks and bumper stickers. Livia grabbed a flashlight from under the truck seat and followed the serrated sound of adult laughter. She tasted acid in the pocket of her throat. She'd be lucky not to puke from nervousness. What a shitty bind she was in, having to face a bunch of strangers with her kind of news. What a shit she was.

She made herself move toward the largest campfire.

They were mostly men, sitting on camp stools or the ground.

She looked for the boy she'd met in Cave Pasture but didn't see him, though the bodies fingered by firelight seemed much like his—slouched and knowing. There were cans and bottles everywhere on the ground, like kindling. She had to walk right into the conversation to be noticed.

She said, "I'm looking for Rory from WilderLands. Please."

There was some snuffled laughter, then a voice said, "You the cops? You the highway patrol?" More laughter. Livia switched the flashlight from her right hand to her left, glad no one could see her crumpling face.

Another voice, sleepier, said, "Rory's up the hill. He likes to get away from these assholes when he can. Who're you?"

"I live down the road. He knows my dad."

"Up the hill," the voice said again.

"Thanks."

She knew the campground well enough to find the path, and she made it as far as the communal water pump before someone overtook her from behind, moving fast. "Hold up. Hang on a minute." It was the owner of the sleepy voice. "You a Pexton or a Flitner?"

"Eaton," she said. "I just need—"

"Rory Van Eglen," he said. "Sorry to mess with you back there. Too much beer and negotiation. Negotiation and beer. That was rude."

She didn't respond. He was tall but indistinct in the dark, and Livia wondered if she could say anything to a guy who looked and smelled like he was made out of smoke.

"You're Paul's daughter, right? I've seen you around. Does he have a message for me, I hope?"

"He don't know I'm here." She could taste Rory Van Eglen's sweat now, on the end of her tongue. It was a tangy, sporty sweat without much animal musk. "It's about that cave."

"Damn cave," he said. "I can see why your dad—why you— would be upset about that. It's enough that people are stupid about the gates and leave garbage on your land, but that cave has been one huge distraction. Your dad's a good man. We can talk land management with him. But now Long Horse and his people want to slow everything down to make their point about cultural owner-ship or whatever, and who can blame—"

Livia clicked on her flashlight, blinding him into silence. "The baby's from Addicoat's. I took it from there and put it in the cave on my own. It belonged to Joe Addicoat and nobody else. That's what I want to say." She clicked off her light.

"Huh?" Rory Van Eglen was bristly necked and wore a tight wool cap that made his skull look small. "Can you say that again?"

She did.

"So you're the culprit?"

"I don't . . . I didn't mean to be anything." A wet and fool-ish sorrow filled her mouth. "That cave . . . it's always been pretty much . . . mine."

Rory Van Eglen began to talk to himself in what sounded like a television voice. He wasn't sleepy anymore. "Well, isn't this the brass balls. Mark Baylor might still be here. And I need to talk to Sally if I can get her on her cell. This is great. The Forest Service thought we were fucking with them, that we'd planted the bones for publicity, but I told them I was only up here about the cows. Goddamn, it'll be good to—"

She aimed her flashlight again. Watched him fishtail his hands over his eyes. "I'm not trying to help you. In case you think that."

He waited until she lowered her beam of light, then blew some air out of his lungs. "Geez. I guess I'm on the wrong team, huh?"

She nodded, knowing he could see that much.

"Okay. Let me stop being the jackass here, Miss . . . ?"

"Livia."

"All right, Livia Eaton. You're telling me the truth? You put the bones in the cave?"

She nodded again.

"And you're talking to me to set the record straight. This has nothing to do with your dad and his grazing lease. You're just clearing up a . . . uh, misperception?"

"Yeah. I just . . . I just dug where I shouldn't have."

Rory Van Eglen yipped through his nose. It seemed to be the way he laughed. "Don't we all, don't we all. I gotta tell you this, though. I admire your good intentions, but folks aren't likely to just pack up and leave. I'm getting calls from Toronto and New Mexico, even one from a Mormon bishop in Utah. People are into mysteries and bodies they can't explain. Everybody's got a story to go with those bones."

"It was just Joe Addicoat's," she said, biting at the inside of her cheek.

Rory Van Eglen leaned toward her until she saw the uncolored refractions of his eyes. "Maybe it used to be," he said, "but it's not anymore."

Back in December, her mother had been well enough to participate in a bird count for the Audubon Society. They trekked west on snowshoes, just the two of them, with Playa paddling through the white wake of their trail. The morning was frigid. A heedless, spiraling wind skated down the icy tongue of the river. Connie said they wouldn't see much, and they didn't. Seven magpies, including the pair that lived in the ranch yard. Nuthatches among the old-growth pine near the spring. An ouzel that frantically dipped itself in a last lid of open water. And the ravens. The ravens bladed and purled the cold, gliding with the confidence of the undiminished and well fed. "They're quite intelligent, you know. They can learn to talk if they want. With real words." Connie removed her woolen hat to watch the heavy black birds joust in the crystalline air. Her cheeks were as red and tender as a child's. "But they mostly choose not to. You really don't want to think about that for too long—or I don't, anyway. How some creatures prefer to lead the life of scavenge."

Hobo's truck was still angled into the willows a mile from the house, but she didn't hear the music until she parked the GMC in the barn. It was her mother's portable stereo. Loud. Livia didn't recognize the melody—it was something shrieky with violins— but she knew what it meant. Connie was up, up, up. Sailing like a kite without a string.

Livia was thinking about how to deflate the situation when she saw a figure standing near the corrals. It was Hobo. He was wearing his work hat but no shirt, and a gun barrel canted downward from one hand. The sodium light from the barn ebbed over his skin, bruising him in blue.

There was something wrong. She could see that much in the collapse of his shoulders. "Hobo?"

"Don't come over here, Livvy."

"Did you get one, a wolf?" Those were the words she said, but what her mind groped at was the obvious absence. Where the hell was her ma?

"You don't want to see." Hobo's voice was cruel and oiled with warning. Livia started forward. Hobo moved to block her path. She tried to fling herself past him, against the rim of darkness that edged the ranch yard, but he fought her into his bare arms. He dropped the gun to do it. It was her Mossberg .22.

"What are you . . . why are you . . . don't *stop* me."

"Think of him like he was, Livvy."

She clawed her way up his chest like a cat. "I have to see, I have to see Ma, let me *see my ma*."

"It's not your ma," he bellowed. "Connie's dancing in the house like a prom queen, goddamn it. She don't even know what happened."

Something unforgiving began to spool itself tight inside her. She was able to hear regular noises again, the fierce hatchet strokes of Hobo's words.

"It's the dog," he said. "The little one. Your dog. We were in there . . . and I thought I heard . . . I rushed it. I made a mistake with the dog." She forced herself to glance at part of his face. What she saw looked swollen and drowned.

"N-Nock?"

"I shot the dog. And he didn't do a thing to deserve it. I'm a damn fool. We thought we heard howling. I was thinking wolf. I was seeing what I wanted to see."

She recoiled from him as if he were a jagged crevice that had just torn itself across the valley floor. Then she began to run. She jackknifed over the fence. Her dog was on his side with his head thrown back and a single white paw folded into the sticky darkness of his chest. She reached out to smooth a pink, inverted ear and felt the warmth that was still nestled beneath his collar. Instead of tears, something appalled began to pour into her mouth. "H-hobo," she croaked. "Why are you even h-here?"

He said nothing at first, but she believed she could smell the sallowness of beer in the air behind her, and she could smell fear, and the stubborn perfume of her mother's burning candles.

"I . . . oh shit, it does no good to lie to you . . . I been to see your ma. She asked me to come, and I knew your dad was up the road in Cooke City. She asked me. I want that made clear."

"You took my gun. You weren't thinking about me or anything else. You k-killed Nock with my gun."

Silence. Then a broken cough. "I said I was rushing. I took advantage. I'll say the same to your . . . to Paul . . . when the time comes. I took advantage. I've always liked Connie. I'm damn sorry about the dog, you got to know that. But I'm hoping I can talk you into giving me some help right now with your mother. She's been running a little hot."

When the time comes. She wondered how a grown man could be such a fool even when he called himself one. *That part of our lives is over.* Her mother was right. Something was finished. In spite of her confession at the campground, she had learned more than the truth on this night. The cold grass that was no bed for Nock knew more than the truth. The high, blind moon that broke its white light across the river knew more than the truth. In spite of her efforts, all she had done was trade one shallow grave for another. All of them had. It was what people did out here. The time for their bitter history was now.

Lost Boys

The garage smells of Sheetrock, the way it has always smelled, and the overhead light that shines on his ropes and his bare legs, his damn bad legs, is harsh. The garage is tidy. He always hangs his tools. The detritus of his field research—redundant grouse skins, the yellow teeth of starved elk—is stored in labeled containers he has stacked on plywood shelves. Linda has never had any reason to complain about how he keeps things. Linda's complaints are more spiritual, or that is what he tells himself. And he won't be responsible for his wife's spirit.

Tonight, he is responsible only for the rack.

Retired from the Department of Game and Fish after twenty-seven years. Father of one son and one daughter, the daughter a theatre major and a known tweaker of meth. His son went ROTC at the university, mostly for the money, and he's just back from eleven months in Iraq with his National Guard unit. Safe. And sound. And maybe that's what this black mood is all about, sitting on a cold, fiercely swept concrete floor, flaking a hundred meters of nine-millimeter rope into a perfect coil again and again. He shot trap with his son, Bridger, just that afternoon; the kid's gotten pretty good, but there was no pleasure in it. The fault's not Bridger's. It's his. He let the damn weakness in his left leg get to him. It affected his lift, his pivot. He let it ruin his aim. All the things he says he loves—his son, good competition, the meticulous cleaning of shot-guns—went to ruin because he allowed it.

He hasn't decided if he'll fight the disease or not. He hates that setup: illness as battle. For now it's more important to refine his thinking just as he did during his heyday in the field. Bighorn sheep. The black-footed ferret. Sage grouse. Managing those species required some serious song and dance. He took his share of hits, even from the governor, but he never quit. The new game warden out of Saratoga, a thatch-haired kid named Jack who wears his red uniform shirt like it's a long-awaited wedding gown, calls him "the wise man." He has that reputation. Patient. A good planner. He was once the dean of state field biologists. Now he's nothing he wants to recognize.

His climbing harness is splayed on the floor between his knees, a blue cradle of nylon and memories. The rack of gear he'll use on the rock lies at his side. Organizing the rack was like threading sweet pearls on a string. His old hexes and tapers are good, always good. He's examined their wires for kinks. The wires are as straight and smooth as needles. He hasn't done a solo climb on the Tusk in a long time, but there are some things you never forget. Flaking the rope has shaken most of the dust from its bright red strands. He can't wait to feel the hot, unforgiving bite of granite against his knuckles. He can't wait to ask his body to do more than it should.

He'll leave before dawn.

Nelson sings to welcome the dawn, though he is shy about it, out of practice. Some of the words are like lazy sparrows in his throat. They refuse to fly. The night has been good, not too cold for the boy, so he kept them both out under the stars, which now sink like bright pebbles beneath the surface of the warming sky. The boy is hidden in his sleeping bag. His hands and knees are tucked against his belly for heat. Nelson continues to sing, humming through the parts of the morning song that don't come to him. He keeps his grandfather's wavery, smoke-cured voice within his ears, as well as he can remember it.

The boy, his nephew, has slept well. Nelson has not, but he tries not to struggle with the restlessness that flutters inside him like a damaged wing. He has fed the boy, the middle son of his sister, and he made a fire with the boy, and he tended that fire while the moon scratched its white claw across the sky and coyote hunted nearby. Nelson's uncle, a veteran of Vietnam and the white man's college in Laramie, says Nelson is too often the nervous bull in the herd. Uncle says Nelson needs to shed some of his nerves with his shaggy winter coat. And so he has on this night. Or almost. He has prayed a kind of prayer. He has smoked many of his cigarettes, their hot ash red against the blue-black of the pines that ring the clearing. He has spent hours thinking of Trina and hours trying not to think of her. He has spent some time thinking about his wife, who no longer has eyes like Trina's. This has led him to believe he and his wife are no longer meant to be married.

As the night wind sowed voices among the pines, he also thought about his sister Donette. Donette is glass eyed and drifty with drugs now, living with a Mexican hombre who deals his poisons right out of her house. Brandon is her son, one of three children she leaves mostly in the care of their mother. Nelson has kids of his own, daughters he worries about. This time with Brandon, a slow walk to a sacred place, is not about worry. Or any kind of big decision. It's about learning what he, and what the boy, can make of an old story.

We aren't supposed to be here. The Tusk and all the headwalls and the whole fucking recreation area have been closed by the Forest

Service for three weeks or a month, some scheme like that. It's a special decree with the Indians. But the weather is so good—it's never this clear early in June, Wyoming weather sucks way too much of the time—and who's going to see us? Who's going to know? Nobody hangs on the western routes, not even during high season. The rock is rotten in places up there, tricky to handle. And there's much better climbing north of Lander.

Henshaw has parked the truck in a righteous place, east of some ranch house on a pullout above the creek so it looks like we're fishing. Damn Henshaw even put fly rod cases in the back of the truck in case anybody comes poking around. He's a joker, Henshaw is. And we're not gonna mess with the rock. No pitons, no fixed bolts. Hell, Henshaw even bought some of that colored chalk that matches the cliff faces up here. We'll be quiet. We'll save the beer and bullshit for later, back at the truck. There's just this one route—one route, maybe two variations on it—we want to make a run at. Nobody's ever bagged it as far as we can tell. It's not in the books, not on the Web sites. But it's there, looking prime with its wicked pitches and angles. Henshaw really wants to post the sucker. And Henshaw is a hellion. So we're in, divvying up the ropes and anchors and water and everything else we need to mule over the hills. Free spirited, just the way we like it. Free.

It's a great day to be outside, it truly is. The predawn sky is as still and unreachable as a distant alpine lake. The foothills east of the house are gray with the beard of a heavy midnight frost. *It's a great day to be outside.* He used to say that each and every morning to Linda when he was on the job, and he meant it. No matter how cold it was, or how stupid the mistake he was supposed to fix, he never disliked leaving the shelter of a roof and four walls. When he was a PhD student trying to radio-collar bighorn ewes, he camped for long, gorgeous, difficult weeks at a time. He had to stand off an old sow grizzly and her cubs—twice—when he was living in that drainage above the Greybull River. The bear had a goddamn insane desire for peanut butter. He swore back then that old age would never tame him. But it has. He lays his pack and ropes in the back of his Dodge pickup in a way that keeps him conscious of the ceremonial nature of the task. Otherwise, the rage sluicing along the veins of his forearms will overwhelm his good thoughts, his tempered attitude. He can't have that.

At the last minute he decides to take Angler, the old Labrador retriever, with him. She was a fine pheasant dog in her day. Her hips are shot and so are her eyes, but she'll enjoy the trip, and there's a chance she'll keep him from thinking too much about Tryon, the collie who used to go with him on climbs when rock was still something he had to conquer.

He helps Angler onto the front seat of the truck. There's a tidal curve of sunlight spreading above the mountains where he first taught Bridger to hunt deer. A six-point buck; he'll never forget the smile on his boy's face. Morning is rolling on its rim. The dog swats her thick tail against the truck's dusty dashboard. It's a good day. She knows no other kind. He rests a hand on the thick, flat bones of her skull as her failing eyes, round and expectant, reflect a tarnished light into his own.

Brandon wants bacon for breakfast. Or pancakes from McDonald's. Nelson reminds him that they won't eat for a long time, not until they've walked to the place they've heard about. I don't want to go, says Brandon, pushing out his lips until he's made his whole face into a stubborn scowl. Nelson knows how to handle that attitude because he tried the same thing on his father when he was a sleepy-eyed boy.

He says nothing. He bows his head and draws the scents of frost and sagebrush and pine duff into his body until they make a kind of map for him. They will find their way. And there won't be a whole bunch of formalities. Or not too many. He's not going to chant this part—not out loud, anyway. Many of their people will be here later in the month to make pilgrimages or cultural statements or whatever they choose to call their journeys. They will come for the solstice, to witness the sun as it begins to shrink beneath the robe of night once again. But this is Brandon's first time. He won't overwhelm the boy.

They set off to the west, up a gentle slope that is thick with red willow, both of them zippered tight into their jackets. The boy doesn't talk now. But he is jittery on his toes, watchful and assertive. He pretends to dribble a basketball past Nelson. He bumps against his uncle's hip, hard. He spins. Then he mimes the action of a three-point shot aimed at the basket of a bird's nest cupped among the willows. He throws both arms high into the air as he scores.

We start late. Holly's hard to roust out of bed sometimes, but what the hell? It's a Tuesday. There's only one ranger assigned to this part of the forest, and she's not looking for climbers. She's got ATVs and dirt bikes to worry about. We don't see any trucks or vans parked at the trailhead, but Henshaw has us leave the road and traverse a low ridge until we get way back in the woods just in case. We don't hear much of anything. Somebody's flying a plane on the other side of the Tusk. I joke that the pilot is scouting for Henshaw's ganja, which Henshaw doesn't think is funny. Some kind of bird is tweeting in the brush. And we all hear the crashing sounds made by deer moving away from us as fast as they can.

We do see one weird thing. Holly finds a ribbon tied to a bush about ten yards off the trail. It looks like a surveyor's mark, only it's not. The ribbon is a piece of red cloth and there's a pack of cigarettes lying at the bottom of the bush, Winstons, and a braid woven out of some kind of green hay. Henshaw says it's sweet grass maybe. The Indians use it. He's seen it before. Holly gets a little tiptoey and hushed when she thinks about what that might mean. She says she'd hate to intrude on some guy who's starving his way into a vision quest or whatever they do up here; it would be a black mark on her karma. Henshaw tells her it's cool. We're cool. It's full daylight. Even the squirrels are obnoxious and loud by now. The important parts of religion are all about dusk and dawn, Henshaw says, the ghosty hours of the day. There's nothing holy about brunch hour. We aren't bothering anything. We're respectful of the earth. It's not like we're littering all over everything or firing guns like some of the local shitheads do. We're just here to climb.

He knows Marian Vargas, the seasonal ranger, pretty well, so he's not going to leave his truck somewhere that will make her curious or piss her off. He takes the forest road at Biscuit Ridge, drives right around the barrier that's supposed to seal off access to the site of the Mule Tail fire that burned a thousand acres two summers before, and parks at the head of a dry wash that has no name he's ever heard. The Tusk is less than two miles north as the crow flies.

The sky is now the gentle color of his daughter's eyes, or that's the connection he chooses to make. Cara was a beautiful baby. She was slow to walk, so slow that Linda worried that something was wrong. He never worried. Cara was just stubborn. He saw that in her from the start. Just as stubborn as her old man. He can only hope she knows what the hell she's doing with herself in Las Vegas or wherever she is right now. Cara has a way of underestimating the ruin a person can inflict upon herself.

Small cumulus clouds roost on the western horizon. It may rain later. There's no fixed trail, so he'll have to go easy for Angler's sake, and that's all right. He shakes the morning stiffness out of his arms and legs. They feel good, obedient and strong. The thing that galls him most about the disease is the cruel and comic way it affects his limbs. Some days he's normal. Some days he has no more body control than a foul-hooked trout.

Water. Harness. Ropes. Chalk. Climbing shoes knotted to the top of his pack. No helmet. He's not going to wear one. He figures it would be damn good luck if he managed to crack his skull open doing something he loves so much.

The air still smells of ash from the old fire. Small yellow butterflies rise from the ground cover that's regenerating on the forest floor. He can see what looks like a goshawk resting on the blackened spar of a scorched lodgepole pine. He files away his thoughts about the climbing ban that's been negotiated with the local tribes just as he filed away the details of a hundred other well-intentioned projects when he collected his golden belt buckle from the current governor. It's no longer his business. His business isn't property rights or politics or the varieties of human respect he was once paid to recognize. He's not going to think about the gripping vise of his own vanities, either. Not right now. His business is leaving the ground.

The boy is thirsty. Nelson can see the lurking shadow of want in his brown eyes, though he asks for nothing. Except singing. He likes it when Nelson mouths a soft tune—something that makes them both a little larger—as they grow hot and tired crossing the dry meadows and steep fingers of forest. It is a long way yet. They can see the rocks, as still as wary animals in the spreading sun, and they can see the purple crown of the adjoining hills and the butte that is honored by their people. They cannot see the caves, or the great height of rock that was split in half by the man who came before them all.

Nelson stops when they reach a cool circle of shade. He strips off his jacket and ties it with Brandon's jacket around his waist. His socks are full of nettles. So are the boy's. He smooths a place for the boy on the ground and shows him how to push the sharp seeds through the fabric of his socks in order to get rid of them. The boy laughs when he tries to brush the nettles off his hands. They don't want to let go. Then Nelson tells a little part of the story. It's familiar to the boy. Most of the children hear the stories—in English and the tribal tongue—at school. But the story is nothing without the attention of the people. And it is nothing without the dark barrier of the hills and the sun's great heat and the towering rocks that can never be taken away. Just a little part of the story, that's all he tells. How Thunder came. And Lightning. The Great Storm.

The boy shows him a place where ground squirrels have gathered a neat pile of pinecones. It's like their grocery store, he says to Nelson. Nelson shows the boy how to find the squirrels' homes—front entrance and back. Then they begin to walk again. The boy fills his cheeks with the fat spirits of the winds. The boy fills his lungs with tornadoes and rains.

He sees them just as he's stepping into his harness, off balance, too much in a hurry. He has one leg up and bent at the knee like a guy getting into his underwear after a quick shower. He knows he looks silly and vulnerable. The base of the Tusk is behind him. The rock is the color of a good chestnut horse. Crystals of mica embedded in the granite wink like jewels in the full-on sun. He's afraid he recognizes the man—the stocky build, the neat braid of hair, the dimpled chin. A nephew of Alfred White Clay? It doesn't matter. He's not supposed to be here. There will be hell to pay, and he'd better get ready to pay it.

Except the man doesn't move. He acts like he doesn't really see a lone white guy rigging up for a climb. He just stands there in the dappled shadows of the crowded aspen grove, his hands hanging lightly by his sides. There's a boy with him, a chunky kid with flushed cheeks and crew-cut hair who's about elbow height to the man. The kid is frozen in position, his arms straight ahead of him like a super-hero in flight, and it's clear even from this distance that he's trying not to laugh.

Peek-a-boo. I see you. To the kid, it's some kind of game.

Christ, what to do? He'll just have to own up, same as he ever has—in bureaucratic quarrels and marriage. It's not his style to make excuses. He fights to dull the pangs of disappointment that spear into his chest. He drops his harness around his ankles. The rack of bolts and anchors rattles like a length of hurled chain. No damn excuses.

Yet when he squints into the striated light of the aspens, everyone is gone. The boy. The man. Vanished. He begins to call out, but stops himself. He's almost willing to believe it was all a hallucination. His brain, as sprinkled with lesions as it is, might be able to put on a made-up show like that. But he doubts it. The kid seemed all too real. His bright, conspiratorial eyes. The laughter.

He looks over his shoulder at Angler, who is sprawled, pant-ing, in a golden quadrangle of sun. She hasn't heard or smelled a thing.

It's a game, sure enough. So he'll play until something stops him. He steps back into his harness. He wraps some tape around his trembling fingers. Makes a nice, careful survey of the first and second pitches of his route up the Tusk. Oh, the stories those rock faces could tell. Pete Davidson slipped and split a kneecap trying to solo up the east side. And that turd of a lawyer, Frosty McNamair, once tore a hole in his pants so big people had their binoculars out just so they could watch his white butt cheeks hang in the breeze while he finished his climb. It's coming back to him like the chorus of a rowdy song—the camaraderie, the bal-ance among partners, the bloody scrapes and falls. That was a life, the whole unplanned rush of it. That was a self no larger than its body. He lifts his chin until the back of his head rests against the swell of his shoulders. It's all up there. Up. History and chance in his muscles one more time.

Spider. Jumping Frog. Brandon does his imitation of those creatures once they have turned back from the place where the stories say the first of their people met Lightning on the great red rock. Crane, Brandon whispers, his dirty fingers cupped around his mouth. That man looked like he was dancing Crane.

Funny crane, Nelson says, grinning a little.

Not too good, Brandon says, the way he does it.

And they both laugh.

Nelson does not know who the man was or why neither of them wanted to talk or explain anything. He knows only that for him the man disappeared. The man did not even leave a true shadow against the rock. It was nothing for him and the boy to bend their path a little. They have left the man to find his shadow. They want to see the caves.

There are others here, knocking against the ancient stones like pellets of frozen rain. Other climbers are here. Nelson knows that, and restlessness flaps against his ribs once again. He closes his eyes. He listens to the *tot-tot-tock* of the bird white men call the flicker. It is drumming for fat insects beneath the bark of a tree. And the wind, it hisses against his skin. The wind can be capricious and unruly when it is close to the holy places. He fingers the bits of red cloth he has stuffed into the front pocket of his jeans. He will show Brandon how to leave tobacco and other offerings in honor of the spirits. And he will make a silent prayer for the boy's mother, just a small one. He remembers Donette's stories of how the women, their aunts and grandmothers and many cousins, walked the old trails up this way when she was a girl, how strange it was, that walking, how surprising. He hopes Donette still holds some of that surprise in her heart.

Spider. Frog. He shows Brandon a few steps of a dance he learned when he was a young one, six or seven hops from watchful Crow. Then they resume their silent journey toward the caves. It has been a very long time since he has visited them, black mouths to another world. The caves frightened him when he was small. He does not think the boy will be frightened. The boy will understand.

We suck. Holly pulls a bad, bad sprain on her wrist when she's got Henshaw on belay, and she's no good for the rest of the morning, and neither is Henshaw or anybody else. Henshaw climbs like his hands have been soaked in motor oil. He rushes everything. He screams at us when he can't snap his hips over the crux at the end of the third pitch. He gets a little wild. The weather is okay—windy but warm—and that's all you can say for the hours of sweat and cussing we put in. It's like we're being graded by some asshole judge. It's like we're being watched from somewhere in the woods. There's nothing relaxing about the assault.

Some days you just don't have your shit together, that's what Holly says. She's got an oozy-looking raspberry on her thigh. And she tells us about a big goddamn raven that flew down and stole the carabiner she had laid out with one of her anchors, stole it right under her very own eyes. Holly doesn't mince words. She mentions a couple of things about karma when Henshaw can't hear her.

But even that guy knows you're an ass to red-point a route when you don't have the proper mojo. It's a fucking mistake to want it too bad. We finally pack it in. And we never see another soul the whole time we're there. Nice surprise when you think about it, all that virgin rock in a no-hype piece of wilderness, so we start talking about how we'll flash the goddamn route when we get our next chance. Henshaw wants us to shut up and swear to some kind of secrecy. He's afraid somebody will make the grade before he does. He wants that rock written down under his name. Typical Henshaw. He thinks somebody is listening.

A cry cuts through the breeze that wraps the Tusk like a warrior's cloak. The boy who hears it might think the red-tailed hawk is teaching her young to glide the updrafts that will launch them into the sky. *Ker, keeeeeer.* The boy has seen such hawks many times. Or the boy might think it is a man who has cried out. Not First Man, founder of his people. First Man disappeared long ago, many years before the bison and the great chiefs left this land. No, this would be the voice of a humble person, someone like his own uncle—a man who wishes to sing about how high his wings have taken him.

The Sin Eaters

July 18 1889
Laramie City to Rawlins
room & board   75¢

The train ride was satisfactory. Porterfield's coach was nearly full,
yet he secured a window seat, which allowed him to examine the
oncoming terrain. Even his passage across the great central plains
had not prepared him for the land he saw. The territory's character shifted rapidly and inexplicably, mimicking the blinking pro-
gression of a stereopticon. There was little logic to the yawning of
the country's dry, broken hills. The only rhythms of the journey
he found familiar were the clacking of the carriage wheels and the
expectant beat of his own heart.

Reverend Morgan had suggested he take note of the site of
Dr. Cope's celebrated excavations. Just a few years before, the
geologist had uncovered fossilized remains of the great lizards

along this very rail line. A gentleman across the aisle was kind enough to mark the dinosaur bluffs for him when the train paused at the Medicine Bow River to take on water.

He had no memorable conversations while on the train, a fact he attributed to his apprehensions. This was his father's trait, a retreat into silence and apparent thoughtfulness when doubt began its assault. Phyllis often reminded him that silence was *not* the equivalent of dignity. He would have to find, and keep, his voice if he was to succeed at Fort Washakie. It would not be enough to speak with conviction from the pulpit. That was a gift he had in hand—he could preach. The truer test of a missionary was how he confined, or mastered, his many human weaknesses. He would need friends in this corner of the West. He would need allies beyond the banner of the church. If she were here, Phyllis would chide him: *You must engage. Share. Reach out. Do not hide your bright lamp beneath a bushel.*

Dear Phyllis, his fiancée. What would she say about this desert land and the rough industry of its oases? Would she delight in the unwavering sunshine of the summer afternoons as he did? Would she compare the marbled fortresses of cloud that crowded the sky to Greek acropolises? He thought she would. Phyllis had an energetic imagination.

The disembarkation at Rawlins was a bit of a jumble. His trunk, of course, had been sent ahead. He hoped to find it with Reverend Langston, with whom he was to dine. He had no trouble securing his smaller bag, but the station platform was a skirmish of travelers, peddlers, newly shipped livestock, and baggage. He was sorry he had failed to cover his collar with a neckerchief, for the wind soon assaulted him with soot and ash from the engine stack. Ah, the wind. Like the distinct landscape he had just traversed, strong winds were a peculiar gift of the region. Laramie City had fairly swayed with its zephyrs. He would be lucky if his collar, one of two he possessed, did not catch a cinder and become singed.

The air smelled of cattle and the cantankerous musk of hogs, which he knew well from his home in Iowa. There was also the acrid stench of night soil from across the tracks where a loose skein of women displayed themselves on porch railings and in doorways. Visible, but unremarked upon, the women mirrored the decorative bunting strung along the facade of the mercantile that stood just beyond the station. Cribs, that was the word used to describe the haphazard structures occupied by such soiled doves. Surely someone in town had the power to eliminate those establishments. Were westerners, at this late date, still so lax? So drawn to temptation? Porterfield clamped his fingers around the cool sphere of his watch case. Wisdom, his father had told him when the man still possessed the full powers of his mind, sometimes depended upon the careful recalculation of judgment. He could not wage the Lord's war on every front. He had not been called to serve in Rawlins. His duty was to the north, with the downtrodden Red Man.

He was not surprised when Reverend Langston did not meet him at the station. He asked a young street arab for directions, and the scamp agreed to guide him to the parsonage. It was a short, dusty walk. Rawlins was not a large town, although it appeared to host the usual potent mix of banks, saloons, and boardinghouses. The boy left him at the gate of a crude, low-slung home without accepting the offer of a blessing. Porterfield let himself through the unpainted gate that was lashed to an equally unpainted post. He checked his coat sleeves and hat brim for remnant ash. Emory Langston was currently the senior minister of the church in the Wyoming Territory. A good impression was essential.

Reverend Langston's welcoming words jangled in his ears like unstrung harness bells. *You have come ahead, brave soul. Despite the prospects, you have come.* The reverend was a tall, bewhiskered man, too tall for the architecture of his home, which was a crooked rectangle made presentable by fresh coats of whitewash and a well-scrubbed plank floor. It was, Langston said somewhat jovially, what the Committee on Missions could afford. And its location near the rail yard kept him in the bosom of his potential flock. He was sorry he could not offer Porterfield a place to rest his weary bones. But his wife had recently presented him with a son, another blessing. There was, he joshed with an open mouth, no room at the inn.

Porterfield's trunk? No, he had not seen it. Surely the station master could be of some assistance.

So he toured the reverend's vegetable garden and its tangle of hearty peas. He visited the uncaulked meeting hall that served the church on Sundays. The fees were low, Langston confessed. On bad-weather Sabbaths they had use of Mrs. Walcott's parlor with its reliable stove. Porterfield did not ask Langston the size or budget of his congregation. The evidence was all around him. Langston spoke with cheerful enthusiasm of his early days in Montana, serving among the piquant miners and their camps. It was all in the spirit, he said. The spirit must never flag. And he was certain young Porterfield had the proper spirit. Dr. Everett had written from Chicago and told him so.

Yet there remained a hesitation, some sort of invisible barrier between them even when he met the sturdy Mrs. Langston and her mewling infant. Langston was all surety on the surface. The breadth of his patience with God's creatures was evident in the way he greeted his neighbors and parishioners. But Langston did not seem as bound to the Word as Porterfield expected. He had an airy, unscriptured way of hewing to his verbal sentiments. He took comic advantage of his unusual height and the abundance of his whiskers. Furthermore, Langston felt compelled to mention that he had made several exploratory forays in the direction of Fort Washakie. The Roman Catholics and Episcopalians were very well organized and financed, he said. The competition for souls was lively. This alarming fact was uttered as a kind of plowman's joke.

His host, Porterfield concluded, had lost some of his nerve.

A small meal of stew and boiled coffee was served. The stew was a watery amalgam of garden vegetables and the flesh of a rabbit Langston himself had snared, but Mrs. Langston was well armed with salt. Afterward, Porterfield led the Langstons in the singing of several favored hymns. The beloved melodies pleased everyone, including the swaddled infant.

July 19
horse, sorrel   20 dollars
Saddle   5 dollars
Overnight at bar 6 ranch

His trunk had been sent on to Lander, much to his relief. After settling with the proprietor of the thin-walled boardinghouse, he aimed himself and his new horse at the prairie. The road was heavily traveled. It was the primary supply route from the Union Pacific line to the northern military establishments. The sociable Langston had assured him he would find good company along the trail. Langston also advised him to put up with the Radfords overnight.

"They are stimulating individuals and eager to converse with learned travelers," Langston noted, his bristled eyebrows cocked in humor. "Radford will attempt to topple your pins. He draws no distinction between us and the Methodist exhausters."

"I welcome the conversation," he told Langston, feeling the mercury bead of his convictions rise to the top of his throat.

"They will feed you to the brim," concluded Langston. "And music you accordingly. They have much to say about this country."

He soon fell in with companions, just as Langston had predicted. He came upon a springless wagon pulled by two teams of spotted oxen and driven by a decommissioned cavalryman who had just had his hair shorn in Rawlins and was all white across his brow and neck. The cavalryman was friendly, and eager with his stories of the Indian wars, but he acknowledged that his team moved very slowly on the inclines on account of their load of barreled victuals bound for the mines of Atlantic City. Porterfield soon left the wagon behind despite the cavalryman's offer of a shared luncheon.

Thinking of Phyllis, he dismounted at midday and chewed at his wrapped chunks of bread and meat in the spindle shade of a lone juniper tree. Phyllis would admonish him not to hurry so, not to rush from the wings of one scene in his life just to seize the stage in another. *Take care not to isolate yourself in labor or in prayer.* He would write to her tonight, he pledged. He would reassure her with his description of the great pale-feathered cranes he had seen dabbing for frogs at a seep. He would tell her how the scant Wyoming rain fell in columns and dried upon his jacket before it even dampened the wool.

Following an unslaked journey across a glaring salt plain, he exchanged greetings with a pair of Rawlins-bound grub liners. The men—rakish, filthy—confirmed he was already riding upon land controlled by the ambitious Mr. Radford. "The Bar Six is a prime outfit," one rider told him. "They run 'em hard and far, and you won't see no fences. Only the damn grangers like a fence. Headquarters is on the river, big as a town."

He did not see the trim rooflines of his destination until the day's sun slotted itself like a coin behind the raw, treeless peaks to the west.

His arrival surprised no one. Passage of the Lord's servant into the wilderness was still regarded as an event, even in these late days. Word of his coming had preceded him. An old man adorned with a green silk scarf that covered the top half of his wart-sprung ears met Porterfield as soon as he rode into the yard. The man did not seem able to speak, but his gestures were keen and practiced. The visitor was to make himself known at the main house. His horse would be cared for. Porterfield wished he were more presentable; he was acutely aware of his own stink. But Christ had been little more than a beggar at times. The Radfords were not likely to recoil from his road-worn appearance.

They did not. He was welcomed, fortified with fresh coffee, and led into a room that held both a bed and a washbasin. Mrs. Radford, who moved with the short-legged confidence of his own Iowa aunts, was a whirligig of tucked skirts and solicitousness. Mr. Radford, she said, was still among his cattle. It was that season. But he and his crew were nearby. They would return for the evening meal, at which time she hoped they might all make a proper acquaintance.

He washed and changed from flannels into a linen shirt that could support his much-abused collar. He penciled a brief entry into his pocket diary before he resumed his study of the Gospel of John. It was not so generous, that gospel, and he was intrigued by its riddles. *Even if I do bear witness myself, my testimony is true, for I know whence I come and whither I am going.*

He was pondering this Christly declaration when a brisk knock on his door summoned him to the Radfords' parlor.

The scene was familiar. The English-style furniture, the bouquet of rosewater that overlaid the earthen smell of roasting venison and onions, the lugubrious portraits of eastern forebears, the prized display of Venetian glassware: these were the same in Chicago and all the fine households he had been privileged to visit. Yet, for once, he was not the supplicant, not the prized young specimen on display on behalf of the perennially underfinanced committee. He was a guest, a stranger. *The zeal of thine house hath eaten me up.* And he had little knowledge of his hosts or their affinity for matters of the soul.

There were three men in the parlor, which had its vast windows open to the cooling temperatures of twilight. Radford was the smallest, although his supremacy was established by his certain posture and the unwavering measure of his gaze. Hogan, a broad-chested Irishman of obviously brooding temperament, was introduced as foreman of some aspect of Radford's far-reaching operations. Mr. Wyatt Ellison was apparently a fellow traveler who had interests in government supply contracts in the region.

"So this is our man of the cloth," announced Radford, producing a vigorous, arrhythmic handshake. "We are honored, sir. You will forgive our crude frontier ways."

"I see nothing in your well-appointed home that would not be cherished in my native Iowa," he responded. His deference garnered some hoped-for laughter.

"Your father is from Iowa then?" asked Radford.

"He is, sir. He led a church in Polk County for many years."

"Ah, a line of Middle West prophets." Radford held to a polite smile. "We may have to improve upon ourselves to equal the expectations of our guest."

"If you aim to civilize the Sheep Eaters on their own patch," interjected Ellison, "tell Radford to fill your soup bowl three times over. You'll need belly for that task."

There was more laughter, though none from the taciturn Hogan.

"I am grateful for your hospitality and advice."

"It is our way here," trumpeted Radford, nodding toward the servant woman who had come to announce the meal. "A vast country. A dangerous country. You will find that we are all neighbors."

The meal was neighborly. Mrs. Radford presided over her lace-covered table with efficiency and good cheer. She urged her husband and Mr. Ellison to avoid speaking of "local troubles" and to offer their guest useful knowledge of the territory. Radford obliged with the mathematics of agriculture: herd sizes, shipping costs, slaughterhouse prices. Ellison showed more passion for water rights and the much-delayed plans for expansion of the railroads. Hogan did not speak. But his hooded eyes remained watchful.

"You must tell Reverend Porterfield of your winter among the Arapaho," urged Mrs. Radford. She spoke softly to the foreman, as if she considered her request a kind of imposition.

"He won't see much of those poor wretches unless he barters with the Black Robes." Hogan gnashed at his portion of venison. "The Shoshone are settled some miles to the west of where the fathers have set up."

"You know the priests then? You've been to their camp?" Porterfield regretted his curiosity as soon as he gave it voice. He did not want to sound too eager.

"I lived only where I could trap and hunt," Hogan said, his shoulders drawn back. "But if you're asking am I baptized in the faith, the answer is aye."

"Hogan is reliable," interrupted Radford, "papist or not. I, however, am of no church at all. Certain zealots want desperately to tame our savages. I am not certain of the point. Are you familiar with Thomas Huxley and his arguments?"

"The last one fled," muttered Ellison.

Porterfield placed both his fork and his knife on the white rim of his dinner plate. "I believe my predecessor at Fort Washakie was felled by pneumonia."

"And your lungs are strong?" asked Ellison.

"I pray for strength, as all men do."

Radford jostled with his napkin. "I prefer Mr. Charles Darwin's ideas to prayer, Reverend. You have my respect. You are brave to leave your Iowa home. But you will forgive me if I do not pretend enthusiasm for your errand."

"It is a calling, Mr. Radford." He tried to hold his host's eyes with his own brimming gaze, but he could not. "The Lord God is not easily dissuaded."

"Chief Washakie's people are known to be gentle," said Mrs. Radford. She stood to pour coffee, apparently hoping to ease the mood.

"They're too ruined to be otherwise," said Hogan, his voice thick with distaste. "We've seen to that."

Mr. Radford convened the gentlemen in the vicinity of his corrals so they might peruse a stud horse Hogan had delivered just that day. The fresh, unconfined air was bracing. The silver hook of the moon seemed poised to lift them all into the net of heaven's stars. Radford's dogs came to investigate the party, and Porterfield lowered himself on his haunches in an attempt to greet them. He did not believe he had ever met with warier animals.

The stud horse was short at the shoulder and hip. His aspect—confident and single minded—was more dominant than his physique. Radford joked about this fact as they all listened to the heated whickering of the mares in their separate pens.

"He's a restless one," said Ellison.

"He needs the devil ridden out of him, and this current business will provide the opportunity," said Radford.

"Then you are going to speak with Averell."

"I'll do more than speak," declared Radford. "The man is a thief and a whoremaster. Hogan brings word that Islington's herd is short. We are all missing cattle. The valley needs a scouring, and it will get one."

"Hear, hear," said Ellison, drawing on a pipe he'd tamped full of tobacco.

"Some advice to you, Reverend Porterfield," confided Radford. "The thing is afoot. Laws must be obeyed. You might wish to stay here another day or so as the roads will be hard used tomorrow."

His fingers searched for the smooth comfort of his watch. It had been his father's. The old man had relinquished it when he could no longer comprehend the meaning of minutes or hours. "I prefer to press on toward my duties."

"Then mark your course for Ferris, if you favor speed. I would accompany you if I could, but I—we—have business. Your departure grieves me. We haven't argued Huxley. Do you know his work on apes? It would do me good to joust with you."

He bowed in Radford's direction, although he knew the gesture was invisible in the dark. "I'm afraid I'm not the sort of warrior you hope for, Mr. Radford. I am untested."

"Not for long, you're not," said Ellison behind the sparking eye of his tobacco. "One month on the Popo Agie River with those wretches will gut you or temper your steel forever."

July 20   vry hot
26 miles then campd

The house was nearly empty by the time he wrested himself from a short, uneasy sleep. Mr. Radford and the others had left with the dawn. Mrs. Radford compensated by playing her accordion while he breakfasted on hen's eggs and cold lamb. She explained how she had learned the instrument at her father's knee. She then wheezed through a mazurka followed by a jig-time rendition of "Battle Hymn of the Republic." The latter, he supposed, was meant to rouse him to song, but he found himself so struck by the ardent pumping of Mrs. Radford's oddly muscled arms that he failed to carry the tune.

He was given simple directions. The old man with the green scarf saddled the sorrel horse and provided him with a packet of sandwiches. He left the corrals of the Bar Six Ranch accompanied by the lusty flute song of larks.

He was not used to long hours on horseback. By midmorning, his buttocks could barely tolerate the friction of the saddle. He dismounted, lashed his jacket to the saddle's skirt, and began to walk. The soil was loose and fine grained. It spilled across the toes of his calfskin boots. The occasional raven dropped from the sky to observe his uneven progress, but otherwise his only company was a series of startled jackrabbits.

He was well forged for solitude. His father—practicing his theories of unrelenting study and cold-weather exercise—had seen to that. This was why Dr. Everett had championed him before the committee. "Porterfield has fortitude. Porterfield sustains himself in our Lord." It was true. He could even now feel a heated gathering of strength in his limbs as he considered the monumental task that lay ahead. *Thou girdedst thyself and walkedst whither thou wouldest.* The lodestone of God's will pointed north.

He sang to himself as the sun rose on its kite string to the east. He imagined sentences for the letter he would write to Phyllis. He looked forward to telling her about the native bluebirds. *They are more feral than the birds so royally ensconced in your mother's trimmed hedges. More cunning, in my opinion. Desperately acrobatic on the wing.* He was so involved in thoughts of the woman he admired, perhaps even loved, that he did not notice he was no longer alone. He was quite startled when his reverie was interrupted by the braying of a mule.

Up ahead, in the sandy wallow of the trail, was a freighter, a mammoth land ship lashed wide with water barrels and graying rolls of canvas. In front of the freighter stretched a veritable regiment of mules, all paired in the traces, all silent save the lone malcontent that continued its honking jeremiad. Porterfield paused to tuck in the loose tails of his shirt. The dark, resinous sides of the freighter wavered in the morning heat. Where was the driver, he wondered. Who would ever abandon such a prairie castle?

His own horse, a suspicious younger mare, solved the mystery by shying backward in response to movement under the askew vehicle. Porterfield ground-reined the mare and made a stumbling approach through the deep sand of the wheel ruts.

"May I lend a hand?" he shouted.

There was no reaction from the figure beneath the heavy chassis. The man was bracing an axle, a dangerous task. The single mule continued to shriek like an ungreased wheel hub.

"Hello," he offered. "Can you use some assistance?"

The driver, his britches black waisted with perspiration, emerged from behind an ironclad rim. He was not a tall man, but his legs made up more than half his length, and they gave him a lean, graceful appearance. His bare torso was corded with the muscle necessary for his profession. Yet it was his hair—rust colored and oiled flat as a trapper's—and the yellow hue of his skin that distinguished him. Porterfield had seen that skin color among the mixed-blood bargemen of the Mississippi River. He did not know how to account for it here.

"I'm Porterfield, Micah Porterfield, bound for Lander and the adjacent fort. Have you thrown a wheel?"

The man inclined his well-formed head.

"I'll help if I'm able."

Another nod. Courteous, but watchful. Discerning.

"Do ye take to a mule?" The man turned aside, his galluses swinging against his heavy bull-hide boots. His voice was battened with skepticism.

"Mules?"

"Can ye abide the creatures?"

"Yes," he said without hesitation. "I have an uncle who trades in mules."

The driver nodded a third time, then spun on a heel and rudely showed the naked slab of his back. "Name's Terpsichore," he said. "She go on my say." Before Porterfield could respond, the man had spidered up the side of his freighter in an apparent search for some tool.

Porterfield covered his mouth and coughed. It was his lone response to the suggestion he join ranks with the mules.

Terpsichore. What manner of man would name a barren creature of toil after the dancer's muse? He looked over his shoulder at his own horse. The sorrel was tearing greedily at a long tuft of golden grass. He reset the sagging shape of his felt hat and attempted to walk with authority up the phalanx of waiting mules.

There were gray mules, piebald mules, mules with bellies the color of fresh cream, fourteen mules in all. Their feet were freshly trimmed, and the hammered rims of their shoes were sealed tight to their hooves. The yards of black harness smelled of lanolin and oil. The animals were clearly well cared for, sleek and fit and unimpressed by his examinations. He could not help but think of his sister Sarah and her bevy of spoiled tabby cats. Terpsichore, a sharp-withered blue roan, was relaxed in her traces. She bore the oversized brand of the U.S. Army on her hip. Her left eye was as marbled as a baptismal font, and Porterfield noted that she wore neither bit nor blinders. Sand flies swarmed among her freckled lashes, yet she maintained a regal posture. The only sign of independence was a rank discharge of urine puddled between her rear legs. The sour flood reminded Porterfield of his own needs, and he had just begun to fumble at his trouser buttons when the driver, a lithe and sulphurous shadow, was upon him.

"Take ye time with her," the man said, foisting an oozing leather bag into Porterfield's occupied hands. "She smart as a Yankee captain." Then he was gone.

The stained and leaking bag, Porterfield discovered, was filled with pungent fly ointment. While the driver tended to the damaged wheel, he had been further relegated to the role of stable boy. And why not? He smiled to himself. Humble tasks were the lot of a good Christian.

He began with Terpsichore, who groaned as he daubed the mess into her long, twitching ears. Her mate, a bright bay jenny whose name he could not imagine, gave no reaction at all. The bay's broad chest was crosshatched with wide, gray cicatrices—signs of old wounds, terrible wounds. He was respectful as he moved past her hindquarters to attend to the next pair of animals.

A sharp whistle arrowed through the air. Porterfield watched as Terpsichore and her fellows moved forward a single step. The harness jangled and creaked. The freighter shifted just enough for the driver to reset the axle within the repaired hub. When another whistle—two staccato beats—sounded out, the teams pressed backward in parade-ground unison. It was an impressive display. The wheel was soon flush and pinned. Porterfield chambered his own uselessness and took the opportunity to empty his bladder in the vicinity of a towering anthill.

"For Lander, are ye?" The mule skinner stepped clear of the sun's flat glare, in hat and shirt this time, his galluses now tight over his shoulders.

Porterfield, still in good humor, produced his version of a mute nod.

"Ride along, if ye wish."

He tied his mare to the rear of the hulking freighter and joined the driver on his narrow wooden perch. The full circle of the horizon was visible from that height. The vast openness of the prospect made him slightly dizzy. The driver announced himself as George Drumlin, contractor for government and industry. He wove three sets of supple reins among his spatulate fingers, and they were away. It was no surprise to Porterfield that the man did not use a whip.

Ribs of wind-polished granite began to emerge from the tresses of prairie. After only a few miles, the rocks resolved themselves into the pedestals of small mountains. Drumlin pointed toward the sweeping undulations of the Sweetwater Valley as the sky boiled itself white with heat. If all went well, they would be along the banks of the Sweetwater the next morning. He queried Porterfield about his mission to the Shoshone.

"Are ye such as can talk to Indians of God and sin?"

"That is my intention. I have studied the phrases of their language. I would speak as one sinner among many."

"What one soweth, another reapeth," offered Drumlin.

Porterfield gave a sidelong glance. It was strangely serendipitous that George Drumlin should quote from the Gospel of John. "Yes. That's so," he said, clasping the edge of his seat as the freighter yawed across a dry gully. "Though we also reap our own foolishness, do we not?"

"Verily, verily, I say unto thee, the hour is coming." There was a deep bass note of reckoning in Drumlin's voice.

"You know a great deal of scripture," Porterfield ventured, "for a man who gives pagan names to his animals."

The driver jutted his jaw into a reluctant smile. "Benedict and Francis," he said, pointing to the matched pair of jacks hitched to the freighter's tongue. "Yonder is Aloysius and Andrew, also monikered for the saints. Betsy Ross had her name when she come to me, as did General Sheridan, the great black one that's just off the lead. The general come by his name honest. He don't like the Shoshone or any Indian." Drumlin laughed.

Porterfield laughed with him. "You are not a man of mere whim, I take it."

"No, sir. I know my place. And my burdens is always with me."

"God's grace transforms us all," Porterfield said, watching a cluster of white-rumped antelope wheel away from the freighter's path. They were astonishing creatures, he thought. One of the Lord's deft miracles.

"I'm afraid grace ain't took with me, Mr. Porterfield. I don't mean to quarrel. I been to my knees, prayed every way I been told. But the devil ain't loosed his grip on me."

Porterfield straightened himself. He hadn't been prepared for a confession, but Drumlin seemed inclined to give one. "Satan *will* be cast out," he said firmly. "A man must only—"

"My daddy's wife used to tell of the cleansing spirits that lived among her people before white preachers come to that tribe," Drumlin said. "She said them spirits visited the freshly dead and eat the black sin from them as maggots will eat at rot. They fed until a body was pure clean, then flied off with their bellies swinging. The dead man was free to pass over." He looked at Porterfield with slivered eyes.

"You prefer such spirits?"

"I seen the signs and wonders, Mr. Porterfield, the signs and wonders. Jesus is a mighty sword, as ye may tell me, but there are human calamities beyond his ken. I have seen them as well. I'd like to be laid clean when my time comes."

Porterfield was silent. He wished to argue, but he found that he could not. He'd had no food or drink for hours. The sway of the freighter seemed to have thoroughly curdled his blood.

Drumlin talked on. He was born on the lower Missouri, he said, to a trader and a slave woman he never knew. His father made his way to the Platte River in the days of the Great Migration and found himself with a kind of steady work on a private ferry near Bessemer. At the end of those travels, George Drumlin had but one sibling left alive—a half brother named Isaiah. Their mixed-breed stepmother was, by turns, cruel and kind.

"Isaiah and me run the ferry a good deal, for our daddy loved his hunts and his drink. We knowed how to figure money, and we knowed the river's moods."

One day a cavalry sergeant and his men rode in from the east. They demanded free passage across the Platte. This was not unusual, although failure to earn a profit meant an encounter with their daddy's fists, deserved or not. The sergeant also wanted to swim his remuda to the other side. This was a rash suggestion. It was late spring. The river was muddy and spasmed with currents. Drumlin told the sergeant there was no need to swim the stock. "Ye can cross them by boat, a dozen at a time." He presented the deal just as his daddy would have.

But the sergeant was scornful and impatient. He insisted his forty horses and mules swim the Platte. Drumlin and his brother and a wisp of a bugle boy were ordered to perform as wranglers so the sergeant and his men could keep their boots dry.

The sergeant hinted they'd be paid for the job. Drumlin demanded more than a hint. The bullying sergeant said he would not reward government money to a nigger child, or whatever he was. He would pay the proprietor. And he pointed a finger at the family shack on the opposite bank.

Drumlin gave in. He and Isaiah had done it many times before, guiding oxen and plow horses from one undermined bank to the next. He sized up the military herd while the sergeant deployed his men on the towlines of the ferry. The animals were a lousy lot, lame with hoof rot and patchy with malnutrition. Drumlin suspected they had been confiscated for resale to line the sergeant's own pockets. He selected a long-nosed dun with a glint of bossiness in her eye. Isaiah legged up on a sturdy brown mule. The bugle boy, who appeared fearful of moving water, clutched his legs around the ribs of a wall-eyed red pony.

The bugle boy was soon swept downstream, separated from the pony as easily as cream separates from milk. Drumlin, the fool, made to save the boy. He was certain he could drag the boy out of the heavy current despite the soldiers' taunts and jeers. And he did. He thrashed them both, bruised and slick with weeds, into the stillness of a back eddy. Isaiah was not so fortunate. His mule panicked when the inattentive soldiers failed to keep the towropes tight. As the ferry lurched downstream, the mule veered toward its swinging hull. Isaiah was struck in the head and slipped beneath the river's bronze surface within sight of a dozen members of the U.S. Army.

"A terrible tragedy," whispered Porterfield, who was embarrassed that talk of a river had increased his own considerable thirst.

"They give my daddy's woman money for a boy who weren't even her own, less than ye would pay for a white child." Drumlin's voice hitched with grief. "She took it."

"You must forgive her that," said Porterfield. "After all these years, surely you can."

"Never blamed her for nothing. Blame is mine. I could have took care of my brother. I could have seen him bathed and buried. I could have done many a thing. As it was I rode off with them damn wicked soldiers. There was a cold that come to my heart that day, it come right from the river. Only twelve year old, and I hired on to care for that miserable herd. Never looked back."

Porterfield opened his mouth, then closed it again. He felt a sharp, sympathetic stab in his bowels. Just before his final trip to Chicago, he had arranged for the confinement of his father at a state hospital. Franklin Porterfield, once a lion of the pulpit, had been steadily degenerated by an inflammation of the brain. He raved. He could not be kept abed except by knotted restraints. He reveled in his own incontinence. Furthermore, he had tried to lay profane hands on his own daughter Sarah. There had been no time for niceties. The papers were swiftly signed. Young Porterfield was expected among the Shoshone.

The hour is upon us.

And so it had been.

They kept to the rough and curving road all afternoon, stopping only to water the mules from the freighter's sloshing barrels. When the first of the evening sparrows darted above the dark script of the harness, Drumlin suggested to Porterfield they share a camp. He knew a place that featured good forage. Porterfield was surprised by the cascade of relief he felt when Drumlin issued his invitation. He had planned to stay at a hunting cabin described to him by Mr. Hogan. "I know that place," said Drumlin, with a pursed smile. "Ye needn't muddy your boots in its bog. I've enough cornmeal and bacon to match your supply of dinner prayers."

As the last of the sun's rays silvered the harsh slopes of the Ferris Mountains, Porterfield set himself to the task of feeding mules from a set of hand-sewn nosebags. The animals' warm, eager breath cosseted his fatigue. He had trouble with only one mule. The scarred bay jenny that paired with Terpsichore would not even test her feed if he stood nearby. Her rolling eyes tracked him as if she expected him—or some other creature—to assault her at any moment. He wondered again at the source of her terrible wounds. Who had abused her with such fury? What had slashed at her shoulders and chest? He waited patiently, at some distance, for her to finish her uneasy meal. Beyond them both, a famished coyote howled its anxious tune.

July 21
River crossing   50¢ meal
Heavy Weather late

The morning was spiced with the perfume of blossoming sagebrush. Porterfield chose to ride separately from the freighter for the first two hours. He intended to discipline the sorrel mare with some hard work. He also hoped the vigorous ride would ease the turmoil that had settled in his stomach overnight. He was not feeling entirely himself.

As they drew closer to the more verdant terrain of the river valley, Porterfield rejoined George Drumlin on the high, shifting seat of the freighter. Drumlin questioned him about his childhood. He seemed eager to hear about Porterfield's heritage and schooling. He himself had learned to read while traveling with the army. He offered no descriptions of his teachers, even when pressed.

The gathering heat of the day began to take its toll. Porterfield wiped real and imagined perspiration from his brow. Twice he asked Drumlin to halt the freighter so he might relieve himself among the prairie grasses. Still, the pangs in his bowels rose like air bladders to press against his lungs. Drumlin talked of Lander, of the great mountains there, but Porterfield could not make sense of the driver's words—the phrases seemed strangely purloined from his own unfinished letter to Phyllis. When Drumlin finally pointed to a low cloud that smeared the horizon to the northeast, the disoriented young missionary found himself expecting the ravenous descent of locusts.

But it was no plague, only a straggle of flyblown cattle driven forward by three men astride three defeated-looking horses.

"Thought to see them kind sooner." George Drumlin sucked at his teeth as he made the announcement.

One of the men approached the slow-moving freighter while his companions bunched the herd on the west side of the road. The air was golden with dust raised by the cows' cloven hooves; their lowing cries ached into Porterfield's ears.

"Seen any boys from the Sun outfit?" the man asked. He maintained an uncomfortable posture on his uncomfortable horse, and spoke from below a pair of nostrils that were cankered with sores. The knot of a ragged blue scarf was tied tight across his bobbing Adam's apple. There were no introductions.

Drumlin shook his head. Porterfield offered that he'd seen no riders since he'd left the Bar Six.

"Can't say if that's good news or bad," the man replied. "I'd feel better if I had these critters far up in the hills."

"Ye driving for the roundup?" Drumlin leaned into his question.

The man stood in his stirrups. He fixed Drumlin with a skulker's glare. "I don't believe I asked you gents your business."

"I'm a pastor," Porterfield said. He'd caught the sharp scent of resentment that hovered over the men and their stock. "I'd be pleased to share a word of prayer."

The man laughed, his pink tongue lolling below his crusted nose. "We got nothing to hide. These cows is branded." And he gestured toward the stringy, mismatched herd stumbling through the nearby thickets of greasewood. "Don't reckon we need a pastor neither. Our souls is sold to the stockyard purveyors. But I thank you."

He paused to peer back over his shoulder. "Got news for you, if you want it. Though I suppose your driver there knows it all before it happens aforetime."

Drumlin did not react to the man's jibe.

"It's a roadhouse just across the river, not two miles away. Woman there sells pie worth your praying."

"Some say she sell pie and more," muttered Drumlin, his hands tight on the reins.

"Wouldn't know about that," the man said, winking. He jerked his horse hard to the right, moving in the direction of his gaunt and slewing bovines.

Porterfield and Drumlin watched the parade pass by. The two did not speak as Terpsichore and her followers rejoined the task of hauling the loaded freighter onward. "Ye'd best go on to Ella's like he said. She sell ye a meal," Drumlin said, after a long stretch of silence.

"What?" Porterfield swatted at a biting fly that had landed on his chin.

"There's no good on this road today. Them boys is driving mavericks. They'll be chased after by the bosses that called the roundup, ones like Tom Sun and Mr. Radford. Ye can cross the river and lay over at Ella's."

"But surely such quarrels don't—" He paused, licked at his sun-broiled lips. Edward Radford had also suggested he stay off the roads. He wondered what his hosts were trying to spare him. "I'd prefer to go on."

"Ye ain't been give a choice, Mr. Porterfield. Ye and your horse need water and shade."

Porterfield blinked. The balloon of his stomach spun with nausea. "Forgive me, Mr. Drumlin. I try your patience."

"Ye've not tried me, Pastor. Ye are the good shepherd." Drumlin's thin lips curled, the smallest hint of amusement. "Have a sup with Miss Ella and Mr. Jim. She a fine enough woman, and a sinner ye can listen to. Her man is a clever feller who knows to watch his back. They won't drag a woman into this mess, no matter what stories is told of her."

"I'm sorry." Porterfield shaded his eyes with a weak hand. "I don't understand. You predict conflict, yet you believe you'll go on safely?"

"There's no call to bother Nigger George and his mules. I got goods to deliver, heaven above and hell behind. Rich men like their deliveries." He shrugged his muscled shoulders.

After a few more moments of unsatisfying discussion, Porterfield eased himself from the driver's seat. He was irritated and woozy. The long drop to the ground resulted in a twinge to one ankle. He could barely summon the manners to salute Drumlin for his excellent companionship. Perhaps an hour or two in the shade would do him good.

The sun, now close to its apex, shone down upon him with the force of four burning planets. He grappled with his water skin and drained it in one unsatisfying draft. The liquid was as hot as English tea. His horse, at least, was pleased to be separated from the dark freighter and its entourage. The sorrel sidestepped and bucked, then insisted on a hard, jarring trot for nearly a mile. Porterfield gripped the saddle's horn until his fingers were numb. The horse stopped when they came to the sluggish trill of the Sweetwater River. The water was still sullied from the passage of the maverick cattle, but the horse drank greedily. Porterfield resisted, his stomach once more on the launch. Though he scanned the blurred and swaying horizon, he could no longer see any sign of Drumlin or his acolyte mules.

After another stubborn mile aboard the sorrel, he spotted the low rampart shape of a human dwelling at the base of a shallow draw. The roadhouse? He rubbed a sleeve across his face and was surprised at the grime he wiped free. Had it only been a single day since he'd tolerated Mrs. Radford's accordion? He could not imagine ingesting a meal, but George Drumlin was right. He needed to set aside the searing crown of the sun. He needed rest.

The log building became an enlarged cabin flanked by two open-faced sheds. There was a cold forge in one shed. There was a scatter of wheel rims and barrel staves in the other. No one came for his mare, despite the insistent sound of that animal's hooves upon the packed dirt of the yard. He slid from the saddle, only to find himself overwhelmed by a swirling ache in his head. His brow went cool and clammy. A fever? Was he taking ill? He fixated on the goal of unsaddling his horse, but his eyes could not clearly sort the buckles from the girth. The boy found him prostrate upon a smeared trample of straw, a victim of the faints.

"Mister? You sleeping it off, mister?" The boy's bare toes dug at Porterfield's neck, nudging hard.

He managed only a groan. Yet within moments a bier of woven arms gathered him up and manipulated him into the cabin's interior space. "He'll be wantin' water," directed a woman's voice. His jacket was removed, as was his hat, which had unaccountably remained fastened to his head. A damp rag traveled across the flushed terrain of his face. It took that ministration to clarify the fact that he was actually perched upright in a wooden chair.

"Th . . . thank . . ."

"No matter, mister. You'll not be the last straggler Gene finds at our door. You've marched yourself a little hard." The voice, high pitched and cheerful, became connected to the floating oval of a face.

"Roadh-house?"

The woman nodded, her gaped smile revealing a stand of well-kept teeth. "That and more. Meals. A bed. Advice. We'll take coin if you have it."

"S-samaritan." He began to see her more clearly—pocked skin, thick waist, a healthy head of dark hair.

"That, too, when it's called for. You should know Gene has done fine by your horse. He's a good child, as good as my own son if I had one. You should be drawin' on water yourself, though. You've not had enough. Then, if it's food you want, we can price you out on that."

"P-pie?"

She laughed from behind her aprons then, a wet bellows sound. "Gene said you come in from the south. You cross paths with Roger Jack and his band of liars? It's no wonder you put an end to your morning with a sick."

After half an hour of hydration and the application of cool cloths, he reestablished himself as Reverend Micah Porterfield of Polk County, Iowa, and the woman introduced herself as Ella Averell, native of Kansas. She tended to her rolling pins while Gene, sty eyed and snot nosed, provided her with split wood, molasses, and flour. She asked about Porterfield's business but seemed unsurprised that he was headed north to bring succor to the Indians.

"I parlayed with a Shoshone band on the river this morning. Starving, they are. And hardly any horses to speak of. Living on roots and dog bellies. But they don't dare take a beef; the cattle bosses would scalp them clean for that. I traded for these." She displayed a pair of beaded doeskin moccasins from beneath the swing of her skirts. "Paid more in cornmeal than I should have, but they can't hunt like they need to. The game is took to the high hills. You might ought to know that."

"I'm told the situation at the fort can be dire."

The woman smacked her large, coarse hands together, raising a cloud of flour. "The situation is hurly-burly, and that's true for every one of us. At least I got a chance to prove up on my land. I been here near three years. Indians made it harder on themselves."

Porterfield tried to gather the frayed threads of his thoughts. What had George Drumlin said about Ella Averell? Was she in sympathy with the cattle rustlers? And the name Averell? That had been impaled on the end of Edward Radford's verbal spears, had it not? Wasn't there an Averell who had attracted Radford's ire? The more he tried to remember of the conversations at Radford's, the more his head throbbed.

"I'm under advisement to avoid all politics," he said.

The woman didn't respond at first, but the boy pushed his wild hair from his eyes and stifled a guffaw. Ella Averell gave the boy a peevish look. "There's no avoidin' a issue when there's men on both sides of it that want the same thing. Land. Water. Gold for their pockets. Way it is here, somebody always gets the shove."

He pinched his eyes closed for a moment and marveled at how sleepy he felt, how uncomposed. "It's not so different in the East."

"I reckon not," she said, "or we'd all still be there. But we're here. Scratchin' at it. I'll feed you a hot lunch if you want."

He nodded.

"It'll be fifty cents, Reverend. Half a dollar for my pie and my irritatin' company."

He was wiping pastry crumbs from his mouth when he heard the urgent approach of a horse. This was followed by a shout and a dash out the door by the boy Gene.

Gene was back through the cabin door before Porterfield could get to his feet.

"It's John. He says they cut our fence."

Ella Averell lifted her head from the task of kneading bread dough. She seemed to grow larger in the relative gloom of the cabin. Her shoulders set themselves as square as a roof beam. "Jackals," she muttered. "Jackals and hounds."

"There's been rough talk at the roundup. That's what he says." Gene hopped from one foot to the other as if the ground beneath him had become heated by coals.

"You help John with that tired horse, then I need you to run the news to Jim. Can you do that?"

The boy pushed at his hair, eyes aglitter. "Yes, ma'am." And he was gone quick as a hummingbird only to be replaced by a taller, sturdier sort of boy, the kind who took time to wash the sweat and dust from his neck.

"They aim to open the whole range, and take every cow they find for their own—mavericks and all. They'll take our stock. Bothwell's man told me that to my face." The boy's narrow chest heaved from his exertions. "There was too many guns amongst them to argue against. Bar Six. Tom Sun. Islington. They was all there."

The woman took two protective strides toward the boy, then paused and waved him into the harbor of the cabin. "My cows carry my brand. Jim'll get into it with the sheriff again, but they got to honor the brands. You done fine. You don't need to count no coup on that bastard lot."

The boy, whose fair hair was shorn as close as a sheep's, turned to the visitor. "I seen a good horse out there."

"This is Reverend Porterfield, John. He's a customer." Her words were clipped and measured. "Mr. Porterfield, this is John, another good boy who's come under my wing."

Porterfield stepped forward, his hand extended in greeting. "The Bar Six?" he asked. "Are you acquainted with Mr. Edward Radford?"

The boy refused his overture and looked at him with bitter eyes. Ella Averell raised both her whitened fists. "An honest answer from you first, Mr. Porterfield. Are you who you claim to be?"

"Certainly," he said from a suddenly scratchy throat.

"Then we got no reason to discuss Radford and his imperial Bar Six. That man wants all he can grab. He don't hold with homesteaders or their rights. You've had your meal. If you aim to ride downriver, you might best amble on that way."

"He should stay where we can see him," John said, his voice cracking under the force of his words.

"I'm no threat, young man. I only rested with Radford for one—"

"Preacher's got his business, John, and we got ours. You gather those calves and get my horse put into the shed." The woman spun on Porterfield, assertive but still smiling. "For four bits you'll get that advice I spoke of, even without askin'."

He ferreted into the pocket where he kept his coins knotted in a strip of flannel. "Forgive my questions. I didn't intend to be rude. You have done me a great kindness."

"All in a day, Mr. Porterfield. All in a day. But we got another matter to attend to at this hour." He felt the kind nudge of Ella Averell's dismissal. "If you ride easy on the river road where John will point you, you'll catch up with your mule skinner."

"Assumin' you can stand a murderin' nigger," the boy said. He was still seething. Seething appeared to be his natural state.

"Mr. Porterfield's a man of God, John. He stands for us all, especially those that ain't clothed like the mighty Pharisees. Mr. Porterfield and Jesus don't judge us by our pasts. You might want to remember that. Has Gene set off to Jim's?"

"Yes'm. He's gone," the boy said. "Art Mills was just behind me on the road. I saw him. He's bringin' the post."

"Good," Ella Averell said. "We'll set him out some pie. Art is a better weather bird than my grandma's geese. He wouldn't have put his ass on that wagon this mornin' if he thought the cow barons was plottin' war."

He followed the road along the Sweetwater River. The Shoshone band Ella Averell spoke of had decamped, but the trampled riverbanks were ripe with the nomad scents of doused cooking fires and excrement. A lone wasted dog, with a tail like a pin curl, fed on something noxious among the weeds. The dog growled and showed its spiteful comb of teeth as Porterfield's horse paused to take in more water.

A war? He wondered at the agitated relations among the few settlers he had met. Would they truly fight one another? And what did the boy John mean by calling George Drumlin a murderer? Was there no one on the roads in Wyoming who was not warped by avarice or crime? *If a man does not abide in me, he is cast forth as a branch and withers.* So spoke the Gospel. Porterfield bowed his head. The withered were much in evidence in this troubled land.

He offered a short prayer on behalf of the hardscrabble Mrs. Averell and the family she'd stitched together. He did so with the taste of chokecherry pie still in his mouth.

He rode forward at a renewed pace then, his boot heels impatient against the sorrel's ribs. His future *must* remain ahead of him. Lost souls lay ahead.

He did not catch up to Drumlin. His first contact was with a so-called bull wagon making the return route from South Pass City. Its driver, a slumped individual whose face was rendered asymmetrical by a grotesque absence of teeth, urged Porterfield to make haste to the next station on the stage route. Bad weather was on its way.

"Have you met Mr. Drumlin and his team?"

The driver worked his misshapen jaw from side to side in weighted silence. His oxen leaned left in their traces, and one of them moaned in a way that recalled a sleeping man pursued by uneasy dreams. The driver spat what Porterfield hoped was a wet white pebble at the loins of the offending animal. "Did," he said. There was no elaboration.

"Is there some commotion among the local cattlemen?"

The driver narrowed his eyes as if he were sighting in a rifle. "Ain't for me or any honyocker to say. You git on to the stage stop where it's shelter. Storm's comin'. Arrow hole in my shoulder tells me so. Yellow George and them demon mules won't be allowed in there, but Lester'll clear a place for you." He spat again—launching another slick pebble into the air just before he snapped the salt-stained reins across his team's stringy shoulders. "Bad storm," he concluded. Porterfield sat mystified in his saddle as the man maneuvered his wagon into a moderate set of wheel ruts. The driver added nothing more except a chorus of curses enjoined to urge his oxen up to speed.

There was no taste of rain on the air, only the grit of sand and seed hull. But the sky roiled to the north. Porterfield separated his jacket from his bedroll and laid it across his knees.

He pressed the sorrel to perform. The mare was less than willing. She did not enjoy surging through the oceanic slaps of wind they soon met atop each ridgeline. Before thirty minutes had passed, the air had become as cool as a root cellar, there was lightning on both flanks, and the foothills ahead were the purple tone of a bishop's stole.

He leaned into the sting of the first lashes of rain. He did not flinch during the sharp, white assault of hail. Onward. Courage. Salvation. His prayers became one-word shouts. He was domineering with the mare as the sky cracked and boomed above them. His hands trembled from an inefficient grip on the reins, yet his thoughts were so radiant, so perfectly forged by the stringent weather, that he did not notice when his horse left the main road for a broad path that led toward an isolated copse of trees. The poor animal craved shelter. She wished to be out of the rain. But he—he was marching. *Thou girdedst thyself and walkedst whither thou wouldest.* He would not have slowed a step if the slim towline of a human voice had not wrenched him from his fixations.

Drumlin. Could it be Drumlin? He squinted behind him through the billowing curtains of rain until he could, indeed, identify the lean figure of the freight driver. The colored man was pursuing him with a desperate articulation of his arms. He wanted Porterfield to stop.

Drumlin stumbled to the mare's side and grabbed harshly at her bridle. He was wrapped in streaming oilskins and his head was protected by a Mexican-brimmed hat. He shouted something incomprehensible as he signaled to Porterfield to dismount. Porterfield swung obediently out of the saddle only to find his horse taken from him before his feet had settled soundly on the turf. Drumlin was running with the horse. Porterfield followed as well as he could, dodging through a thicket of what appeared to be fire-blackened timber. Drumlin was madly urgent about something. Fear of lightning? If so, it was a worthy fear. The sky was low and white veined with electrical pulses.

He tasted the acrid bitterness of wet ash on his tongue, and wondered how he had ended up so far from the main road. The grove of trees looked almost impenetrable now that he was on foot. The ground was oddly springy beneath his boots. It made a strange hollow sound as he ran. Twice, he fell hard across the black-stained boles of destroyed trees. As Drumlin and the horse outpaced him, he began to suffer an unsettling panic. His skull filled with an unfamiliar invading hum. His bare hands became oddly heated. But he kept his gaze fixed on Drumlin and the thrashing hocks of his horse. Before long he was on firmer footing, able to wade across the flooded canal of the road toward the south-facing incline where Drumlin had stowed the freighter against a shallow sandstone cave.

"Ye safe up here," huffed Drumlin, as he unsaddled Porterfield's mare with enviable speed. "Out that grove. Out that foul suckin' sand. Lose ye horse in that place."

"Pardon?" Porterfield dug into his freed saddlebags for a pair of hobbles for the sorrel.

"Ye was in a tainted place," said Drumlin. "Looks to be good cover, but it ain't. Believe what I say."

"The horse wanted to go there. I didn't . . . I wasn't even . . ."

"Believe what I *say*, Reverend. They's bones aplenty where that sand takes its grip. Ye'd have lost this horse. Maybe more."

Porterfield wiped his face on a soaked sleeve. "Then I thank you. And I apologize for my ignorance. It's been . . . it's been quite a day."

Drumlin hurled Porterfield's saddle under the freighter's belly in one powerful motion. He said nothing more.

"There's something else, isn't there?" Porterfield read the tremble of agitation across the mule skinner's shoulders. "I felt it, Mr. Drumlin. I was filled with the Spirit as the Lord sent down his rain and thunder, and I gave the mare her head. I was . . . distracted. But I felt it just the same. That grove *is* a black place." He took his battered hat from his head as a gesture of appeal. "Are your spirits in those trees? The ones you spoke of—your eaters of sin?"

"No." The man struck Porterfield's sorrel fiercely on the rump and sent her toward a large stone overhang where his mules stood gathered with their tails set against the persistent wet wind. "Suckin' sand is all that riles me. Ain't no sin eaters in this valley. They couldn't abide the place. People hereabouts won't honor what's clean in a man. People here got no name for sin. One of Dull Knife's braves told me it's a hole in the ground near that grove. It sucks like the suckin' sand. It steals the hearts of warriors, swallow it right out ye chest. That's what he said to me." Drumlin tucked his britches into the tops of his boots. "I need my heart."

"Yet here we are."

Drumlin did not speak as the thriving storm sluiced the air between them. Porterfield began to understand that the driver had summoned a great stock of will to come to his aid, that it had cost him something private and sacred to do so. The man's sacrifice twisted between them like a badly woven length of rope. Porterfield heard again the deep warning hum within the bones of his skull.

"You've saved me from something, haven't you?" he asked.

"I don't know what I done, Reverend," Drumlin said finally. "Nor why. They's no more travel for me today, that's a fact. My load won't sail this mud. Ye can go on, if ye so moved. Lester will take ye for the night at his stop."

Porterfield held Drumlin's stubborn gaze. "I'd rather not. I am not of much use to you, I realize that. But I can maintain a fire. If you'll not go to Lester's, then neither will I."

The red-haired man produced an indeterminate grunt, but his face was not unwelcoming. "Ye horse has took to my children. I reckon there's no need to limit their companionship." He waved to where the sorrel had inserted herself into the tribe of mules. "Nor our own. Ye've not traveled this territory before, Mr. Porterfield. I need to recall that. It's wrong of me to fault ye mistakes too much."

The brute center of the storm whirled south, leaving creeping fingers of mist in its wake. The mules relaxed their vigilance and began to graze downslope of the freighter. They moved in and out of the mist like apparitions. Porterfield noticed that none stepped in the direction of the burned grove. He tried to examine the place from a respectful distance as he gathered firewood. In the sated light of evening, the delimbed ebony trunks looked no more threatening than a harbor's thicket of boat masts and spars.

He extended his hands before him, hoping to feel the unmoored chaos he had felt before. He wanted to touch it again, know it, to meet it with his Christ. For surely that was the test—to be able to match all other powers with God's own force. Alas, now that he was ready he felt nothing.

He helped Drumlin stake a length of canvas at an angle against the freighter. As they squatted to watch their coffee boil, Porterfield told George Drumlin what had transpired at Ella Averell's roadhouse.

Drumlin's face took on the hard, pale cast of alabaster. "All who are in the tombs shall hear his voice," he quoted. "There may be killin'."

"You think it likely?" Porterfield measured the dread that suddenly invaded the cavity of his chest. He didn't like to think of Ella Averell with only two ragamuffin boys for protection. "Murder. Over a cattle dispute?"

"Human killin' has its history, here and in every place I have ever knowed." Drumlin shut his gold-flecked eyes. "I never saw my daddy alive again after I left with that cavalry remuda. Never heard how he ended. Never asked after him. A new man had the ferry when I next come to Bessemer, and I never said to him who I was. Who I *been* had no meaning on that merciless river. Ye hear what I'm remarkin', Reverend?"

Porterfield thought of his own father. Authoritarian. Soiled. Scholarly. Without dignity in his last days. "You suggest there's little in this world that holds men accountable. You've said so twice now. I beg to differ. A man's soul in Christ's hands—"

"I stayed with the white man's army," Drumlin interrupted. "Didn't wear the uniform of no country, nor give pledge to any general nor chief. But I stayed with the army, and I tended to its creatures. I signed the ledger for hell, just the same. I done things. They's blood on *these* hands, no matter what's been writ to Jesus."

"So you . . ." Porterfield wet his tightening throat. "So you have killed men. Yet I believe I sense contrition. There is forgiveness for all of us, especially those who take up arms in a right cause. All you have to do is ask. The Lord offers his grace to those who must sometimes go to war."

"Ain't no sometimes about it, Mr. Porterfield. We at war. We always at war—inside or out—every day of our lives." Drumlin skewered him with a glinting, unsheathed glance. "Ye need only look deep in ye own self to know that."

July 22
poor weather contd
Meal at Lester's—travel N. w/ Stage party
Lander tomorrow

He slept. He did not recall closing his smoke-glazed eyes. He did not remember saying good night to George Drumlin as they unrolled their damp blankets beneath the freighter. He was awakened by a strange feline yowl of fear and, as he rose to his knees, he saw—dimly—a wide, imbalanced shape swaying before the orange platter of the fire. Drumlin appeared to be wrestling with an intruder.

"That'll do," hissed Drumlin. "Stop ye foot stomps and bitin'. That'll *do*." He acknowledged Porterfield as he clasped the invader tightly to his chest. "I heared him comin'. I knowed his horse, knowed the sounds of its gait against the ground as did my mules. It's young John from the Averells'."

Porterfield could barely distinguish the boy from his captor, except for a pale swatch of the boy's light-colored hair.

"Plow horse he was whuppin' is half dead. He say he ridin' for help. He say they hung Jim Averell as a rustler today, and they may have done for Miss Ella, too."

"They did. She's kilt. She's dead," the boy wailed. "I seen what happened to her."

"Who?" Porterfield yanked the braces of his pants over his shoulders. He could not keep the shiver from his voice. "They hanged the woman?"

"On his say they did," wheezed Drumlin, maintaining his hold on the boy. "He ridin' for his life 'cause of what he seen. What men like ye friend Edward Radford done in the name of commerce. He reckons he a blood witness."

Porterfield tried to calm the thumping of his heart. "We can't be certain what's happened without investigation. I can leave now and speak with the authorities. I can—"

"Hear what the boy says, Reverend. He ridin' for the law in the next county since what sits on the throne in Rawlins can't be trusted. This ain't no stage opera with a laughin' surprise at its end. This is money rule."

"Can we escort him then? Is that your plan?"

Drumlin shook his head. "I can't take nobody nowhere in this mud. His horse needs a blow. And the boy hisself needs rest. He half out of his head. I say we corral 'em both. Ye hear me, young John? Ye layin' up. If any man follows ye to Nigger George's camp, they got to deal with Nigger George."

The boy gave no response. Porterfield could not contain his gasp as Drumlin squared the child's shoulders and struck him hard across the face with the flat of his hand. The boy cried out, then sagged into the mule skinner's arms. "Ye dealin' with Nigger George now," he repeated. "Ye all are."

It took Porterfield a long, shallow moment to find syllables for his tongue. "Mr. Drumlin, surely—"

"Ye watch him, Reverend. Watch like he Christ the Lamb hisself. I got to tend that horse." Drumlin dropped the boy to the ground as if he were a wet sack of flour. He stepped in close, his eyes without light. "He'll want to run on ye," Drumlin whispered. "Just like a animal. Ye must stand firm. Terpsichore and Nigger George will track back a ways to see what on his heels. That mule works like a hound when she smells a stranger."

Porterfield struggled not to recoil from the driver's hot breath. There was lust in the other man's words, lust and the great weight of resignation. George Drumlin was transformed. He pitied anyone who came upon the driver in the dark.

"I'll watch the boy," Porterfield said. "But I ask that you show restraint."

"And I ask that ye get in ye boots," Drumlin said, speaking with raw impatience. "I pulled 'em off ye some hours ago." He moved toward the freighter and rummaged among its cupboards until he had a rifle, cartridges, and a rope. "Got a notion to manacle our visitor, Mr. Porterfield. I don't believe he one for genuine hospitality."

Porterfield moved to Drumlin's side. "That cannot be necessary. Think of what the boy's been through."

"I think of no man, Reverend. It's poor luck we been drawed into this. Some will see us as takin' sides. I ain't ready to be cut down by the bosses. Maybe ye is, but I aim to keep ahead of what comes my way. It's my devil nature."

The boy had struggled to his feet. He stood still as a statue in the blue-rimmed hour of the night. Drumlin approached him as a carpenter would approach a length of milled wood and struck him again. As the boy crumpled to the ground, Drumlin grasped his wrists and expertly bound them together. "I receive not honor from men," he growled. "Ye will die if ye leave here, young John. I swear it. Either them boss men will slit your throat or I will." He then hitched the boy to one of the freighter's giant spoked wheels. He did not speak again before he slipped into the gloom with his rifle. Though the mules remained as silent as scouts, Porterfield could not help but think of Drumlin's scarred bay jenny and the possible source of her cruel wounds.

He tried to coax the boy to sit on a folded blanket while he worked to revive the fire. "We should hold out hope, John. Mrs. Averell may be fine. The Lord rewards a cheerful heart."

The boy gripped his roped wrists across the top of his head as if to squeeze what he'd seen right out of his skull. "She's kilt, Mr. Preacher. I seen her face swoled up to black. She fought 'em, damn 'em to hell. She fought 'em so hard." His voice gummed up with tears. "You need to let me go, Preacher. I can't stay here. I promised little Gene I'd git help. There ain't nobody to look after Gene."

"You can keep your promise. Mr. Drumlin has a plan."

The boy looked at him with scoured eyes. "You must be more of a fool than Ella guessed if you're trustin' of that nigger's plans. His only plan is murderin'. You heared him. It's what he likes." He yanked hard at the rope knotted around his wrists.

"Stop that," Porterfield said. "It's for your safety."

"What do you know about keeping safe? You laid in a feather

bed in Edward Radford's palace house. You camped with a piss-colored nigger who does what the bankers and buyers say. He's a man killer, if you didn't know. Drowned his own brother in the Platte River when they argued over coin. Shot army prisoners in the back without no need. Ain't a decent person in the valley who trusts him."

"You are suffering a terrible grief," Porterfield said patiently. "I want to help you. Mr. Drumlin wants to help you. We should seek our strength. Do you know how to pray?"

There was a short breath of silence followed by the sound of muted sobs. "I can pray," the boy said. "Been doin' it since Ella rescued me from my drunken pap."

"Then let us ask his blessings for Mrs. Averell."

He brushed a spot smooth for his knees and knelt near the boy, who—after a brief delay—imitated his posture and the modest murmur of his voice. He would never know how much time passed. Prayer always lifted him out of time. He knew only that he did not hear John slip to his feet and grasp the solid length of firewood that he used so well as a weapon upon his captor's head.

When he came back into himself, he was still partly on his knees. His eyes whirled with the bright colors of city lights, the Chicago gas lamps that had glowed over his departure some weeks before. He thought, for a moment, that he was back on those streets, serving some errand among the urban poor. There was that sort of clamor in his brain. His mouth was stringy with a burning, bitter vomit. His eyes were blind with tears.

He was still retching when Drumlin slipped into camp aboard the ghostly shadow of the mule Terpsichore. "The boy softened you, did he?" the driver said. "I reckon ye can stand."

Porterfield shook his pulsating head.

"He took ye horse, which shows his wits. But he'll stop at the wrong place and somebody will sell him to the bosses for a palm crossed with silver, which shows wits ain't enough. He not likely to see the end of the week."

"They . . . they will kill him?"

Drumlin said nothing

"I . . . I am so ashamed." Porterfield did not even try to raise his face.

"It's ye lot, Reverend. Ye wish to live by the way and the light. Won't no man dispute ye intentions, not even on this godless plain. But ye no more than one fly among thousands on this damnable hide."

"Please don't torment me, sir. I have failed here. I admit to it." The pain in his head was wide and hot now. It spread as thoroughly as a mantle across his wretched shoulders. He thought of Phyllis and her small, silk-slippered feet. He thought of his father's wasted, spasmed limbs. "Do you foresee more failure then? Is that what you wish to claim—that there is no chance for the salvation I seek to deliver to the people of this place? You stand in a position of proper judgment, for I have been foolish. Yet I refuse to see you as the demon that others speak of."

George Drumlin produced his own braying laughter. "I ain't the high devil, Mr. Porterfield. I got a bad nature, it's true, but temptations ain't my gift." The mule skinner squatted low, his rifle barrel aimed toward the black mat of the sky. "Let not ye heart be troubled. Chief Washakie and his people won't find no fear in the way ye do things. Go on. Go and build ye four-walled church. Ye have the gift for that. Be done with me and that wandering boy and them bloated bodies swinging from a tree. Be done with this warring land of greed and toil. Find what makes ye a good scripture story in that fort town with its proper people and proper streets." He lifted his hollowed face to the obscured sky once more. "Ye just got no business finding it here."

Acknowledgments

These stories were originally published in the following journals: "Border" in *Ploughshares;* "Brief Lives of the Trainmen," "Oil & Gas," and "Lost Boys" in the *Idaho Review;* "How Bitter the Weather" in *Five Points;* "The Little Saint of Hoodoo Mountain" in *Shenandoah;* "The Sin Eaters" in *Copper Nickel.*

I discovered my ghosts in many places, including archives at the Albany County Public Library. *Ghosts on the Range* by Debra D. Munn and *Indian Legends and Superstitions* by the Pupils of Haskell Institute also provided source material. Plutarch's short biographies of Roman heroes nudged me toward my treatment of trainmen.

Ella Watson (Averell) and James Averell were lynched in the Sweetwater River Valley in 1889. Some of the characters in "The Sin Eaters," such as the boys John and Gene, are very loosely based on historical figures. Others, such as Reverend Micah Porterfield,

Edward Radford, and George Drumlin, are products of my imagination. It is true that a group of politically powerful landowners were linked to the lynching. It is also true that a Protestant missionary was in the area at the time and stayed overnight with a rancher who was probably involved in the misdeeds. Furthermore, most of the witnesses to the lynching subsequently disappeared. No one was ever convicted of the crime.

The Ucross Foundation and the University of Wyoming offered me wonderful support. The staffs at the American Heritage Center and the Buffalo Bill Historical Center were also extremely helpful. Connor Southard urged me to write a ghost story or two. Bob Southard organized the palliative fishing expeditions. Jane Dominick made it possible for me to write at the incomparable 7D Ranch. Katie Dublinski never wavered in her generous beliefs about literature and its value. Thank you all.

Alyson Hagy was raised on a farm in the Blue Ridge Mountains of Virginia. She is the author of three previous collections of short fiction and two novels, *Keeneland* and *Snow, Ashes*. She lives and teaches in Laramie, Wyoming.

Book design by Connie Kuhnz. Composition by BookMobile Design and Publishing Services, Minneapolis, Minnesota. Manufactured by Versa Press on acid-free paper.